CONFESSIONS OF A
BLACK SUMMER

CONFESSIONS OF A BLACK SUMMER

To: Diane

Enjoy the Journey
of Love, Lies & Drama

Always
C. D. Ringgold

Constance Danielle Ringgold

Rev. date: 06/11/2014

With the barrel of the Beretta pressed against his temple, I knew that there was no turning back. My decision was final when I realized that Brian had no intensions of leaving or letting me go. I had to do something. I stood over him as he slept, trying to figure out the reason behind my ever loving a man who is so nasty, cruel, spiteful and resentful to me and my children, and for no apparent reason. He'd put me through so much, and with all the years of bullshit piled on me, I was officially at my breaking point.

With each passing second, my skin crawled with rage. Making this a painless death would be too easy for him. I needed him to suffer like I've suffered for so long. My finger forcefully rested against the trigger as I closed my eyes to stop the burning. The only fear that was running through my veins was for my children, because they were going to be without a mother and father, very soon. The sweat continued to run from my forehead, blinding me. I was already living in my own personal jail, so I was ready for whatever came next.

Everything flashed back, causing me to sob silently. My thumb eased the hammer back with a deafening echo that sounded throughout our entire bedroom. I swallowed hard, but the jawbreaker-sized lump still remained.

"God, please protect my babies and forgive me for what I need to do. And send this bastard's soul straight to hell," I prayed in a low whisper.

Both hands shook violently, but I never lowered the gun, and he never moved an inch. That nasty son-of-a-bitch looked peaceful, after all he'd put me through. I shook my head; if he only knew what was coming his way.

I closed my eyes, squeezing the trigger. My heart pounded in my ears; suddenly something began tugging at me. It couldn't have been my conscience, because it was on my side. The tugging continued. My vision was shadowy, but what I could make out in the midst of my haze was that it was my sign from God.

"Mommy, it's okay . . . I still love you." Miranda's comforting voice confirmed as she remained by my side.

I began crying even harder. This was an image, I didn't want for my daughter, so I lowered the gun in the darkness. As I led my guardian angel back to her bunk-bed, I turned around and glanced at Brian as he snored even louder, mocking me. Our daughter, the one he never wanted and questioned for five years . . . had just saved his miserable life.

WINTER *2009*

1

As I answered the phone, I heard, "My husband gets on my damn nerves." Before Solae continued, I played the conversation in my head because it wasn't going to be any different from the ones that I'd had with her before. I sat down on my blueberry Chintz ottoman, letting the phone rest on my shoulder. I wasn't in the mood to listen to anything she had to say, but I prepared my brain for the useless information that I was about to receive.

"What happened?" I responded.

"I'm pregnant! That's what happened!" she yelled allowing her annoyance to take precedence over the situation. "Little do he know, he's gonna' be looking like the damn fool because I'm getting rid of it," she laughed uneasily. "I already got my twin investments, and as soon as his brats turn thirteen, I'm out of here. The way I see it, I'll have ten years of marriage in by that time, so I'll get half of everything and child support. I'm set, but in the meantime, I have to do me, and that sure as hell doesn't include another baby." she said sucking her teeth.

I gasped. I didn't realize how ratchet my best friend Solae Roberts was until now. Or was she always like this, and I just chose to ignore it? Either way, it was pathetic, even for her. Instead of expressing my feelings immediately, I paused before I said something that might cause an unnecessary argument.

Deciding to break the silence, I questioned, "Is this what you really want to do? I mean, I just think that you should give this some more thought."

"Please! I have never been so sure about anything in all my life. Besides, I didn't call you to pass judgment on me like your life is so damn perfect!" she attacked.

After I remembered who I was talking to, I brushed off the fact that I couldn't take what she said to heart because this was her, one-sided. A few deep breaths exited my mouth, and I brushed off the fact that she could manipulate any situation into her favor. So like any other time I backed down.

"That wasn't my intension . . . I'm sorry." I said apologetically.

"Anyway, what I really called you for is my dilemma." she informed me.

I released a soft, sarcastic laugh before I had a chance to stop it. I wondered what she meant by her *dilemma*. But I didn't question her about it or what she thought she had just told me. There were so many issues: Her husband had gotten her pregnant and she didn't want to keep it, yet she was disregarding the situation like nothing had happened.

"I'm gonna' use your place tonight." she told me.

"For what?"

She huffed through the phone as if I was, in some way, inconveniencing her life.

"Because nosey, my boo Brian was coming over. But thanks to my good-for-nothing husband coming home to spend some time with me, I need to change my plans ASAP. If Daniel thinks that he is going to ruin my Valentine's Day, he has another thing coming." she screeched.

"You are crazy! What am I supposed to do while you're using my place to cheat on your husband?" I asked.

"I'm not really sure, and I really don't care. I just can't see past getting mine tonight." she said bluntly.

If she could cheat on her husband constantly and use the twins without any remorse, then this was definitely the response I should have expected but nonetheless didn't appreciate.

"Wow, that's how you really feel?" I asked.

"You can't just do this for me? I'm so stressed out, and I need this so bad. I haven't been with Brian in a week. I've been so miserable and Daniel hasn't been making things any easier me. For instance, this morning that white bastard served me breakfast in bed. The bacon was pork, the eggs were soft boiled, the bagel wasn't raisin cinnamon, and he had the nerve to put milk in my tea!" she sucked her teeth. "First off, I don't like pork on my fork, and secondly, he knows that I'm on a strict diet. To add insult to injury, he had the nerve to buy me a two-and-a-half carat-solitaire-promise ring. The gesture made me sick to my stomach . . . it was yellow gold! Gurl, my morning has been pure hell. On top of all of that, he had the audacity to call and let me know that he was taking me to Atlanta for dinner. News flash, I won't be here when he gets home." she laughed boldly.

"But you married him." I said in respond to her *underprivileged* life.

"I didn't have anything else better to do at the time. Besides he has money and good credit all of the things that are hard to come by in a man these days." she confessed.

"It's crazy!" I yelled mockingly.

"I know right." she responded seriously.

There were no words for a person like her. Solae subconsciously loved men that dogged her. Now that she had a good man, she treated him like leftover scraps, finding nothing wrong with her behavior. In my opinion, Daniel was better off without her. Secretly, I envied her for trapping the well-off mortgage broker that worshipped the ground his mocha-trophy wife planted her *Louis Vuitton* pumps on. I just wished I'd be as lucky.

"What time is this supposed to take place?"

"He should be on his way now. I'm waiting on my cousin to come watch the kids. Entertain him until I get there." she dictated.

"Wait, who said . . . ?"

"I know you, you're so predictable." she interrupted.

What annoyed me even more was knowing that she viewed me as one of the weakest links in her platinum chain. Was I predictable enough to allow her to control me every chance she got? Her true feelings took our relationship to an entirely different level, now that I was finally acknowledging the truth.

"For a person that has as much mouth as you, you always need my help. But that's beside the point. I had my night planned, and it didn't involve me leaving here."

"I don't have time for this drama. I need to get dressed. I'll be there as soon as I can." she said disregarding everything that I had just said.

My eyes roamed from the fifty-inch, back to my plush sofa. Instantly I became irritated because my night was supposed to consist of *Lifetime* and Cookie Dough ice cream. Now I had to figure out something to do before they arrived.

I flopped down on the pistachio-draped bed and looked up at the ceiling. Her happiness wasn't benefiting me, so there wasn't any reason why I was uprooting my life for a person that had everything that I wanted. Then again . . . .

The doorbell rang repeatedly and didn't faze me or move me from my position. He knocked hard, forgetting about the bell this time. Any normal person with sense would have left after twenty-minutes of standing out in the cold, but he didn't. His persistence reeked of desperation which was particularly unattractive. After a few more minutes passed, I got up from my comfortable bed and went to the door.

My hands rested on my curvy hips and I waited for him to speak. When he didn't say anything, I stepped back to shut him out. Then, I heard his deep voice echo in the freezing air, "You must be Mia. Solae has told me so much about you."

He stood in front of me lying because I wasn't familiar with the Solae that gave anyone else the spotlight. And on top of that, his abundant confidence annoyed me.

"Did she tell you that I don't approve of her doing this?" I asked pointing to him.

I had him figured out already, and his cockiness was not welcome in my house, no matter what Solae had to say about it. Instead of waiting for rejection, he took it upon himself to step inside. I shook my head at his direct boldness.

"Sure, come in." I said cynically.

Brain removed the solid-black scarf that was wrapped around his neck and took off his Cashmere coat. Impressed with himself, he made sure that I noticed his six-foot tall, well-maintained cocoa physique.

Damn! I now understood why Solae was risking her marriage. I bit my bottom lip plotting out what might be under his dark clothing which were hugging the muscular parts of his body. I let out a deep breath because I needed to get past the physical. I fought my freaky thoughts. If only he knew what was running through my mind. I forced myself to erase the images I was battling because I couldn't do this all over again.

"Mia, the best way to describe me and Solae's situation is *don't knock it until you try it.*"

Brian winked at me.

He had the wrong woman if he thought that I was going to fall into his lap. I turned up the light so that he wouldn't get the wrong impression.

"What is that you have on?" I asked diverting his conversation.

"Why, do you like it?" he responded.

"You know what? You're cocky for no apparent reason."

He rubbed his bare face and laughed.

"Thanks for noticing, but I don't think that you would have commented if you didn't like what you saw."

That comment wasn't even worth a response from me, so I flagged him off.

"I need to see how long Solae is going to be 'cuz I gotta' get outta here."

He laughed and licked his lips seductively before I walked away.

From the kitchen I watched his every move. I fanned my face with the rose dishtowel because he was doing it for me. Breaking my intense thoughts I took out my phone and texted, *Where r u?* While I waited for her response, I poured a glass of *White Zinfandel* and joined him in the living room again.

"No thank you, I don't want any." he said shaking his head this time.

I crossed my legs and continued sipping.

"That's good to know because I didn't offer you any."

My phone vibrated against the glass-end table. I picked it up and read the new message shaking my head.

"What's wrong?"

"She wants me to entertain you until eleven! That ain't gonna' happen. I didn't want to spend this much time with you let alone . . ."

I looked down at my watch.

"Two hours and forty-five minutes. Hell no! Not gonna' happen! I'm sure that you can find something else to do until she gets here. But I'm going to need you to find that something else, somewhere else."

I put the glass on the table and headed to the door. Opening it I let the February chill inside. Brian looked over his shoulder. With an amused look on his handsome face, he told me that he loved every second of my attention. I extended my hand towards the door and said, "I'm serious, you can come back later."

"Why are you so mean?"

"That shit just didn't really come out of your mouth in my house?"

"It did . . . but I truly believe that it's a mask to cover up something much deeper."

"Oh, so on top of everything else, you're a Shrink? You know what, don't even answer that. I don't want to give you any more reasons to stay where you're not wanted."

Brain was in my face, like he knew me, which was making me tense. He removed the door from my hand, secluding us from anyone that might interrupt these fiery moments. I refused to look at him, but he didn't allow that. In all of his dominance, Brian took his hand and forced me to make eye contact with him. Things were definitely getting real.

"I'm not mean." I whispered.

"I know deep down, you really aren't. Just misunderstood and unappreciated."

He moved the hair out of my face, and I relaxed. This moment was a replica of how things started between me and Solae's ex-boyfriend. He told me the right things at the right time and I gave in willingly. And now, here I am again, in the hot-seat being tempted.

I shook my head.

"Tell me that you want me to leave." he said rubbing my cheek.

"I . . ."

Brian traced his finger across the exposed parts of my upper body. When he pecked my raspberry tinted lips, that gesture caught me off guard. I now knew that we shared the same feelings so I didn't hesitate to let my guard down so that he could come right in.

"Don't . . ."

Brian's soft lips landed on my neck giving me erotic chills while his hands began caressing parts of my body that had been neglected. Despite the waves that I'd be making in my friendship by not stopping this, the feeling was too good to resist. I was officially torn between loyalty and pleasure.

"We can't . . ." I mumbled.

My mouth was saying one thing, and my body was screaming hell yeah! I was going to get mine now and deal with the consequences later.

He unbuttoned my shirt as each perfect kiss starting making its way from my neck down to my belly button. His tongue, warm and fat, licked my exposed breast.

"We can't do this." I managed, but I didn't stop him.

Brian looked up at me with his large-brown eyes. My sweaty hand clutched the cherry-wood entertainment center, and his dark wavy head. I braced myself when his lips kissed mine. My moans vibrated throughout my dwelling, breaking the silence that I would have been forced to embrace tonight. I didn't realize how bad I needed the touch of a man . . . too bad it was this one.

I removed the sweater from his body and threw it across the room. Brian's force moved me against the beige wall as he gripped the back of my neck.

"Oh shit!" he yelled. "You still want me to go?" he mocked.

I put my hand over my mouth to silence myself. Trying to prove that he was the shit, this man took me through the motions physically and mentally. The reminder constantly pounded in my head leaving me feeling good about my predictability. When my tired body slid to the floor, I just stared at him without saying a word. It was worth it.

"What's wrong?" he asked trying to catch his breath.

"I don't even know anything about you . . . and we . . . ."

"I'm thirty-four and married with no kids. I'm a Cleric at Deliverance Worship Center. I've worked for GGW for seven years and I love women." he smiled, proud about what he just revealed to me.

"A Minister . . . , isn't this frowned upon?" I asked pointing between the two of us.

"I'm not perfect, that's why I named my church, *Deliverance*. See, I used to hustle, boost, you name it, and I done it. But to me the church is the new hustle. People spend their last dime to gain favor with the Pastor. It's legal and nobody gets hurt."

He squirmed uncomfortably.

"Discovering this game has put me in a different tax bracket. This one sista' named Felicia would do just about anything to be with me. She didn't care 'bout me having a wife. She just wanted me. Felicia even got rid of her fiancé, the only man that was ever in love with her . . . for me," he continued stroking his own ego. "I didn't have any intentions on being with her, and she had to know that by my actions. It's not my fault that she chose to ignore the signs. Felicia sold her house and all her inherited acres and bought me a Lincoln SUV and Jaguar convertible. She gave me practically everything that she owned. I'm talking about the finer things in life: trips, clothes, handmade custom robes. She even put me through school. That masters degree in psychology sure does come in handy in this hustle, and it works."

"And what did you have to do?" I asked.

"I did what I always do. I sold her a dream, and when she couldn't pay for it anymore, I snatched her world right from under her." he told me.

Before he continued, he hunched his broad shoulders and shook his head arrogantly.

"She was, without a doubt, the ugliest woman I'd ever seen in my entire life. Felicia was five-feet, 280 pounds. Her hair was like sprouts of Brillo pad, she had ashy molasses skin, bugged eyes and feet that looked like hooves. But once I worked my charm, that country-mud duck thought she was some celebrity. And her ass . . . . Woo! It was this wide . . ." he said gesturing with his hands.

Brian's cold, disturbing cackle sent the hairs over my half-naked body on edge.

"But she could cook her ass off. Her chicken and dumplings were mean." he said excitedly finally giving her minimal credit.

"Where is she now?" I asked, but quickly regretted that I had engaged him further.

"Last time I heard, she was in Moreland Rehabilitation Center. She had a nervous breakdown. That led to her stroke on account that I had sex with her sister." he added normally.

"What!" was the only response I had for what he just said.

"You heard me. I'm not ashamed of anything I've done, doing, or gonna' do. Some stuff I wish that I had done sooner. Besides Aura was gorgeous as hell, and the sex was some of the best I ever had, except for you." he grinned slapping my cold thigh.

Remembering his past, he detached from reality, and a satisfied look appeared on his face. The fear of becoming another one of his victims made me sick to my stomach. When I was in the moment, I'd felt damn good about myself. It felt even better because although Solae didn't have a clue about what just happened, I finally found vindication in our relationship. But something that was supposed to add a little spice to my dull life was turning out to be a disaster, if I let it. Solae finding out what went down tonight wasn't going to be anything compared to what Brian thought he had planned for me. What could I really say because I was just as wrong as him.

This situation had trouble scribbled all over it; he slept with family members and ruined lives all in the name of the church. Felicia was stupid for getting caught up in the way she did. I wasn't going to let Brian catch me up like he did her. I knew how to get what I needed without getting hurt.

"Say no more." I said.

"Where's your bathroom?" he asked.

I pointed.

"Down the hall and to the left."

The doorbell rang at the same time that Brian came out of the bathroom. We made eye contact establishing we would say nothing about tonight's occurrences, and I opened the door. Solae walked past me as if I didn't exist, leaving her soft scent lingering behind.

"Hey babe, sorry to keep you waiting." she said kissing him on the lips.

I smiled. If only she knew where his lips had just been. Brian hugged her tight disregarding everything that had just went down between us. How quickly he forgot.

Solae and I grew up in the same middle-class environment. I had to work for everything that I had while she had everything handed to her. This time wasn't any different. She took off her waist-length-grey sable and laid it on my reupholstered chair. Placing her hands on her slender waist, she showed off her backless teal dress. Solae rested on one of her silver gator heels which showed off her toned legs. Her flare always got her plenty of attention, wherever we went, and that pissed me off.

Her face was perfectly made up as her freshly polished diamonds reflected under my insignificant lights. I looked down at myself feeling self-conscious about my current situation. I smoothed the imaginary wrinkles out of my tights and button-down shirt. Now that she was finished with her dramatics, she threw her three-hundred dollar Remy over her shoulders, staring me up and down with distaste.

"Ugh, you look horrible . . ."

She dug in her bag.

"Here, take this money and go get your hair done or something."

It wouldn't have been Solae if she didn't make me feel irrelevant.

2

Ever since I met Brian, I haven't been more uncertain about my three-year situation. Before that night, I couldn't see past Jeremy, but now I was looking over him to the next best thing. Brian hadn't showed me anything spectacular, but I still wanted what I knew that he possessed and exactly what he was giving Solae. At this point, love had nothing to do with what I wanted. Rather, lust and money was ruling my decision to keep this going.

I moved closer to the edge of the bed, so that he couldn't touch me. He just couldn't take the hint, especially after I'd been telling him for the past two weeks that I've been on my monthly. Jeremy wasn't taking care of business at home, and neither was I.

What I didn't need him to do was wake up, so I gently eased out of the bed, taking my phone with me. I didn't bother looking back at my boyfriend, sleeping unsuspectingly.

"Wassup stranger." I said easing the bathroom door closed.

"Who is this?" he asked.

I sat on the side of the bathtub, as the smile on my face disappeared. I was feeling some type of way because he forgot about me after the night we spent together. But tonight if possible, I was going to make him remember.

"Mia . . . remember?" I asked hoping that he wouldn't say no.

"Mia . . . . Mia . . ." he fumbled.

"Solae's friend . . ."

"Oh, that Mia. It's late. How did you get my number? Did something happen to Solae?"

"Actually no, she's fine. I've been thinking a lot about you and our night together."

"Really? I haven't given it a second thought because it was so long ago." he said coldly.

"It hasn't been that long ago. It's been close to a month." I replied feeling a step below scum.

"Anyway, how did you say you got my number again?" he said not letting that question go.

"I didn't, and I rather not say. But I see that I caught you at a bad time. It won't happen again." I said to end the declining conversation.

"So you said that you've been thinking about me? All good I hope." he said relieving some of my anxiety.

"Yes it is." I said meekly boosting his ego.

Although the door was locked, I kept my eye on it. I didn't need Jeremy to find out anything, any sooner than I wanted him to know. So I needed to get my bid in with Brian before Jeremy interrupted me.

"Can we hook up?" I said coming straight to the point.

"When?" he asked without resistance.

"Well, there isn't anytime better than the present."

"That can be arranged, but what's in it for me?"

"What do you want besides me?" I asked with a sudden burst of confidence.

"Sweetheart, I don't take pussy payments. I can get that free from anybody. Cash is always better."

I laughed at what had just come out of his mouth, but he was dead silent.

"You're serious . . ."

"Yes I am. I'm going to text you the address."

I didn't know what to think about Brian's request. I had a man lying in my bed who only asked for my love. Was I really about to pay for a few hours of pleasure with a married man who I'd borrowed from my best friend? I sat stone still, contemplating what move I was going to make tonight.

I was always the person that cared about what people thought about me. I wondered how Brian would view me after

I approached him with the money that he had asked for. At the end of the day, would he consider me to be some weak and pathetic female that had to pay for a man's attention? There was only one way to find out.

I crept out of the bathroom, holding my heels and bag under my arms. I really didn't care that things had come to this point in my *committed* relationship. Being with Jeremy wasn't giving me anything but hard feelings. Now, I had to do me.

I knelt at the foot of the bed, and took his wallet out of his jeans. There was only a ten dollar bill inside. I sucked my teeth because chump change irked me to my soul. This type of stagnate lifestyle was exactly why I was sneaking out. It was time for me to cut my losses and move on.

"Mia, where are you going?"

He sat up straight in the bed at the same time that I had one foot out of the door. I was going to respond, and was damn sure that he wasn't going to like my answer.

"Out . . ."

Jeremy turned on the bright light staring at the clock.

"It's four a.m." he informed me.

"What's that suppose to mean to me?"

"I'm just going to come right out and ask you. Are you cheating on me? I mean that's the only thing that I can think of. Lately you've been distant, nasty, and unavailable. And now look at you, dressed like a whore and sneaking out in the middle of the night." he insulted.

Jeremy got out of the bed wearing nothing but a pair of stripped boxers. Physically he was making me nauseous. I can't believe that I was once in love with him at one point in my life. Now looking at his short, aging, French vanilla body, it confirmed that I made the right choice for the evening.

"The last time that I checked, I was grown, and your name sure as hell ain't William Latham. And if I was you, I would watch what you say out of your mouth. Have you stopped to think that maybe you're the reason why I'm sneaking out of the house in the middle of the night? So since you asked, it's a possibility that tonight I am going to see another man. What I need from you, is to be gone when I get back."

I stepped out of the car trying to calm myself down from the argument I just had with my dude. When I saw Brain's lights flashing, I walked over to him and got in his car. As I tried to form the right words, there was a brief moment of silence.

"What took you so long?" Brian asked.

"Well, it's nice to see you, too."

"I know it is. So, what is so important that you lured me away from my wife at this time of morning?"

"Now, I'm not so sure . . ." I responded.

Commenting on his wife turned me off but not to the point that I was willing to walk away from him. There was still some potential buried deep beneath this deception.

"Let's try to keep the wife comments to a minimum."

"You have my money?"

"What are you, some sort of male hoe?"

"I never looked at myself as a *hoe*. But nothing in life is free, so you have to do whatever it takes to get what you want out of life. I gave you the first taste free, and now you have to pay for more. Its just that simple."

"Maybe this was a mistake on my part coming here, calling you . . ."

"Wait, you don't have to go just yet. Let me get a few things straight first. If you want me to be a part of your life you have to get used to certain facts. I'm a cold-hearted asshole that always gets what I want. But remember this, if you don't want to give me what I want and need then some other woman will." he announced.

Brian's words numbed me. I had too many expectations for a man that wasn't willing to give anything but take everything. The sad thing was, I knew that if I did things differently than all of his other women, then he wouldn't give me the time of day.

"I hear you loud and clear. Now let's do what we came here to do."

I decided to settle for what he was offering and that was borrowed time.

"No money . . . you can kiss this goodnight." he said putting my hand on his business.

I shook my head because I went from one extreme to the next. So far, this night wasn't turning out the way I expected it to. I opened my wallet and shook my head. I'm glad that it was too dark for Brian to see my facial expression of repulsion. As I counted the burning twenties in my hand, I handed Brian two hundred dollars. He counted the money and laughed in my face.

"Who do you think you're spending the night with? Some corner-boy from around the way? Don't insult me with this toilet paper ever again."

3

All I had on my mind was Brian to the extent that I became obsessed. Having sex behind his job and paying for it cheapened the moment for me, and caused me to doubt what I was doing. Brian acted like I should have been satisfied by the fact that he made time for me, but I wasn't. My entire motive for doing this was ruined because I unintentionally caught feelings for him. So, now I needed to find a roundabout way to get into his mind in order for me to be his number one. Inviting Solae to lunch was going to allow me to learn more about him and put me in the position to win his heart.

"I haven't seen you or talked to you since Valentine's Day." I began.

"Yeah, I've just been so caught up with Brian. I only make it home to get changed and run right back out. Hell, I don't even spend time with my kids." she boasted proudly.

"I see that you are really taking this one serious."

She shook her head. Solae had a glow that I hadn't seen in a long time.

"I am because it is serious. You know how I am. I get bored easily, but this one does it for me. I'd even leave my husband to be with him." she told me.

"Why? I mean what is so special about him as opposed to anyone else including your husband? The question you have to ask yourself is, *will he leave his wife to be with you?*" I asked.

"That's the thing. It's not about him being special. It's about him being him. Don't get it twisted. Brian is no different than any other doggish man out there, but I'm in love with him. He does take some getting used to, but once you get past his hard, selfish, lying, hoein', scamin' shell, he's not that bad to be around. And as far as him leaving his wife for me, that's not necessary if he keeps laying the pipe the way he does," she laughed. "See I got this just because." she said holding out a white-gold bangle draped from her wrist.

And all I got was screwed in a parking lot and I had to pay for it. I shook my head.

"There has to be more to it than what you're telling me. What are you doing to get him to give you things?"

I was skeptical about what she was saying, so I was waiting for the uncut version.

"By being submissive. You know that I'm not, but I play that role to fit the role."

"You mean to tell me that by being submissive, you got that?" I questioned.

"Not just that . . . also trips, money, banging ass, sweaty, crazy sex."

She licked her lips remembering her freaky nights with my dude. I shook my head hating the fact that he was still dipping in her bowl when he had me.

"Yes . . ." I agreed relating to the sexual aspects of her story.

"What?" she asked.

"Oh nothing. I'm just agreeing that any woman would love to come home to that."

Almost giving up my secret affair with her former dude suddenly silenced me. She made their relationship sound like paradise, and I wanted that too. I was going to get it now that I knew which game to play.

"And you just met him?" I said still in disbelief.

"Who said that? That's what you assume. I been with Brian for a year, so I put in my time."

I looked inside of my wallet at Jeremy's credit card. If the gifts that I was going to buy Brian wouldn't win him over, then I was going to go back to the drawing board until he was officially mine.

"Shit, I know all too well," Solae said with a smile on her face. "But I know one thing, I'm going to do anything to protect my position." she said with conviction.

"I'm in the mood to do a little shopping."

The moment I got rid of Solae, I dialed Brian's number. I was nervous because I wasn't sure who I was going to get this time. But what I was willing to pay to get him was limitless.

"I have something for you." I said.

"You don't think that you gave me enough last night?" he responded.

This was Brian's half ass attempt at modesty, so I ignored it because he didn't mean it. I had that feeling that he fed all of his females this same line.

"Flattery will get you everywhere." I said playing into his mind game of submission.

"I'm glad you feel that way. Whatever you have, you can bring it to my place."

Brian's unexpected offer caught me off guard. Internally, I laughed because he was so full of shit. And the worst part about him was that he was so unpredictable. I didn't have time to process his madness, I had to give him an answer before he changed his mind.

"Do you know who you're talking to?" I asked, trying not to get my hopes up too high only to have them crushed.

"Yes, Mia. And I want to spend more time with you. What I haven't seen in a long time is potential in a woman and you have that trait." he fed me.

All of a sudden, I didn't feel that the expensive watch and the five *Polo* sweaters were gifts of desperation. Although I was anticipating this episode and he made it a reality, I kept reminding myself that what I won't do, another woman will. I didn't have room for errors.

"Since you put it that way, I'll see you soon." I said without delay.

Just for my reassurance, I looked down at the paper I had scribbled his address on. This was the real deal because any man with something to hide wouldn't knowingly bring me to his place, knowing that his wife could walk in on us at anytime. If he didn't care about his vows, I wasn't going to worry about them either. At the end of the day, the damage was already done so if she had any issue with me seeing her husband, she needed to take that up with him.

Marble floors, chandeliers, gold trim, Persian-area rugs and leather sofas decorated the lobby of Ogden Towers. This place looked better than some people's homes, including mine. Seeing where he lived only increased my need to perpetuate a fake image just to a fit into his world.

"Can I help you, miss?" the oversized man asked.

I swung around, leaned over the marble-based counter, and peered at the guest log. I pointed to my name on the sheet.

"Okay, you can take the middle elevators to suite 813 West."

"Thank you."

I nervously waited until he came to the door. When he snatched it open Brian motioned me not to say anything while he was on the phone. I shook my head in compliance, stepped inside, and shut the door behind me. Everything around me was dreary which was not what I expected from a man with an over-the-top personality like his. What I was seeing compared to what he was showing me wasn't adding up. It was cold and impersonal, and I didn't feel wanted. Although he invited me over, he left me alone to finish his conversation with his side-piece. I checked my watch. If I wanted to sit on a couch alone, I could have stayed at home. I got up, went to the door that he disappeared behind, and listened.

The truth was always there, if you looked for it. My heart broke when I heard Brian tell her that he loved her, and that he had something special for her. I couldn't deny what I just heard, so I refused to let my heart acknowledge it. When he said goodbye, I ran back to the deep mahogany sofa and crossed my legs.

"This has been an interesting evening. I didn't come here to stare at your walls. I came here to spend time with you, but I can see that wasn't part of your plans. I'm good, and I know you are too so I'm going home." I shot at him.

"That's fine by me. Text me to let me know that you got home safe."

The initial shock of his disregard hurt deeper than I could explain. Instead of responding, I picked up my bag when he grabbed at it.

"Before you go, don't you have something for me?" he asked instead of telling me to stay.

"I did have something for you, but now I rather return it."

"That's really childish!"

"No, it isn't. Leaving me alone to talk to another female and expecting me to be happy about it is childish, Brian!"

"Damn, I invite you into my home, and you invade my privacy . . ."

"Are you serious right now?" I asked.

"Yes, and don't sit here pretending like you didn't know that you weren't the only one."

"I know but damn! You don't have to flaunt it in my face every chance you get."

"Damn, you don't have to be so damn sensitive," he mocked. "If you want this to continue you're going to have to toughen up, relax, and let me be a man and do what I do."

"If that's the case, stop flaunting your bitches in my face, and when I come over let it always be about me. And I won't have to be so damn sensitive." I said.

"I guess we have a mutual understanding because I want your life to be about me. Now what do you have for me?" he asked again.

I handed him the bag and sat down beside him.

"Do you like it?" I asked as he examined each piece.

"I love it, but I have something that you're gonna' love even more."

He pretended not to hear my last demand, so I nudged him with my knee to get his attention. There was no way in hell that I was going to let this subject die, so it was in his best interest to answer me.

"Babe, if I wanted nagging, then I'd be here with my wife." he said turning his back to me.

"What did I say to you earlier? I don't care about her, so don't bring her up around me."

"If you stop acting like her then I'll stop comparing you to her."

"All that I'm asking you to do is leave your wife! You acting like I'm asking for a kidney or something. And break it off with Solae."

"Are you serious?" he asked facing me.

I shook my head yes.

"I can do that . . ." to his response, I smiled. "But first you have to prove to me that you have the capabilities of being with me. Prove to me that you are worthy of me leaving my wife and Solae for you. I'm willing to, but why should I?"

An inquiring look came across my face because I needed to know exactly what he meant by *worthy*.

"What do you mean by worthy? Haven't I shown you who I was and what I can do?"

"Um yeah, but you are inexperienced. Besides, there's always room for improvement. And boo, don't assume that the gold mine between your legs is enough." he said humiliating me.

I didn't know how to take what he just said. I thought that I was doing a damn good job with what I was given. This was my first-married-man scenario, so I was going with the flow. But now, I was starting to doubt the man that I fell in love with.

"Oh really? There's something you need to know . . ."

Brian raised his eyebrows.

"Just because I'm young doesn't mean I'm stupid."

"Babe I know you're not, and that's why I love you."

Did he just say that he loved me? I said nothing as I processed that statement. He took our sexual relationship to an entirely different level, and it just proved to me that everything that had happened up until now was worth it.

"Now that we got that established, I wanted to show you something."

Brian reached in the oak nightstand and pulled out a magazine. He placed the marked page open on my lap.

"What's this?"

"Your devotion to me. I want you to get a truck for me, in your name. And in a few months, transfer everything over to my name. You can still maintain the payments. I won't take that from you."

"Why?" I questioned.

"Because this will show me how much you're really invested in me and this relationship. How much you are willing to sacrifice for me? How much do you love me? I'm not in the business of hearing how much you love me. I need you to show me. And to answer your question, my money is all tied up in investments. So do you love me?"

4

My downfall is that I'm generous to a fault. Instead of saying no to Brain's demand for a truck, I stayed up all night stressing about the situation. I was trying to find ways to delicately approach the subject without making him mad. On top of everything else, I had to deal with his empty threats to leave me, and I could do without them.

"This is the one." he said rubbing his hands across the shiny-black truck which sat on a Benz' showroom floor.

I didn't say anything because I couldn't get over the huge price tag that was attached to loving this man. Maybe I should have said something, but now that we were here, it was too late to back out now.

"To be honest, I'm not settled on it. It doesn't fit you."

"Actually, I really didn't want your opinion. I was just being nice. My mind is already made up," Brian paused. "Oh, I see what this is. You trying to back out. I don't have time for your juvenile games. When you're ready to step up and be one of my women, then you give me a call." he said shooing me away.

"No, I'm sorry. I'm going to do this." I said with doubts.

The paperwork sat in front of me while I initialed the new car smells and signed on the dotted line. While I was dealing with the overwhelming details of the transaction, I suddenly developed a migraine. I held my partial-tuition check of nine-thousand dollars in my wet hand. Before I knew it, my money was gone along with my education. Now it hit me, Brian could walk away at anytime and leave me with nothing. That unsettling thought consumed me as he squeezed me only after taking the keys. He shook the dealers hand, and I knew that two people benefited today.

From this day forward, Brian had no reason to question me about anything. I proved my love for him when I walked into the dealership and signed my life over to him naively. I couldn't tell him that I can't afford the $550 a month to keep him riding in style. Brian had high expectations, and I needed to meet them, at any cost. Even if it meant me living in a cardboard box.

I pulled up behind him in front of my apartment complex and got out of the car. I walked up to his window and waited for him to finish his call that lasted from the dealership until now. Only after he was done he rolled down the window. Gratitude wasn't obviously in his vocabulary.

"Aren't you coming inside?" I asked.

"No, I have something else to do." he said.

After I gave up my money, he couldn't even give me the evening which would be free. I'm sure everybody had their price, but this truck wasn't his. What did I just get myself into?

"What is so important that you can't spend time with me?"

"Don't start your shit!" he snapped. "I was with you all morning, and now I'm gonna' handle my business!" he yelled.

"That wasn't for me. It was for you."

"Whoever it was for, we was with each other."

"Damn Brian, who is it this time?" I asked showing the fact that I was hurt by his choice.

A dark cloud suddenly formed above head spraying a misty rain on me.

"You said you was going to end it! I kept my end of the bargain, now what about you?"

"Don't ask questions about things that you really don't want to know the answers to."

"I'm not letting you leave until you tell me something or stay with me." I said reaching into the truck to grab the keys.

Brian was rebelling against me, trying to keep me from taking the keys out of the ignition. He turned his body, blocking me while he pushed me out of the window with his elbow. I jumped onto the hood of car, holding onto the wiper blades. He got out and slammed the door causing the truck to shudder.

"Listen, get the hell off of my truck! Just because you bought me this damn thing doesn't mean that you own me!" he yelled. "You think that you did something big by doing this, you sadly mistaken. I could have gotten any other female to do this, but with you, I didn't have to work for it. I laid it on you real good and you gave it up!" he announced.

He grabbed hold around my waist and pulled me off.

"Maybe so, but I'm renting you as long as I'm spending my money on you. And you need to tell me why you won't stay!" I said as tears rolled down my hot face as a result of his honesty.

"I tried to spare your damn feelings, but to hell with it! To hell with you! I'm spending the night with your best friend Solae! Hands down she's the better woman for me! She has more class than you'll ever have in this entire lifetime! There it is, black and white! Dumbass!"

I watched him speed away while I sucked in the fumes of his fifty-thousand dollar gift.

I dug myself deeper into debt. Maxing out my credit cards to keep up with Brian and make him happy left me hopeless. My stress was mounting because Jeremy slipped a note under my door telling me that he was coming to see me at one. I knew what this was about, so I needed to find a way to justify running up his credit cards to support another man.

The first knock on the door was ignored. But when he started calling like he was crazy, I finally got off the couch, put on my blasé attitude, and answered.

"Wassup?" I asked not letting him inside.

"Are you going to let me inside, or you got that dude in there?" he accused.

"Listen, what I do with my life and in my place is none of your damn business."

"The same place I signed for you to get?"

"That's beside the point. Tell me. What do you want, Jeremy, because I'm not in the mood for your shit either!"

"Oh, you finding out that the grass is not greener on the other side?"

He knew exactly what I was up to. That had never been classified. I didn't feel bad for the way I was treating him because I just wanted him to go, and I would say anything to accomplish that

"You know what, I don't even know you anymore. You're a stranger to me. You're lying, sneaking around, stealing from me . . . you don't even know who you are. You trying to be like Solae, but you will never be her! Find your own damn identity!" he snapped.

Jeremy was a bold-faced liar. I'm glad that I found out now who I was dealing with before I wasted anymore of my time. I tried to tell him in many subtle as well as direct ways that I didn't want him, but he didn't want to accept it. My last alternative was to treat him like shit until he got fed up and left me. I couldn't wait till that moment came because it might have never come. So I had to force him out. He was just mad that I knew who I wanted, and it wasn't him.

"Wait a damn minute! I've been called many things, but a thief isn't one of them. And now you are calling me a Solae imposter! You just mad 'cause I don't want you anymore."

Now that things were playing out like this, I don't feel bad for running up his cards. But technically, I don't consider what I took from Jeremy stealing. I just took what I needed from him for a good cause and for the years I put up with his boring ass. I was over it, and I think that he should have forgotten about it and moved on.

"Then how can you explain these charges for two thousand dollars?" he said holding the statements out for me to take them.

Little did he know, there were more charges coming to him.

"Listen, get outta' here with that dumb shit!"

"Wait we not done! You owe me, and I'm not leaving until I get some answers and my money!" he yelled.

I shut the door leaving him outside of my place acting a fool.

5

My mind was far from doing any type of office work today, but I needed the overtime especially since a text from Brian informed me that I'd be purchasing twenty-five hundred dollar rims for the new truck. I was still pissed at the fact that after I bought him the truck, he chose to spend the evening with Solae. Now I was broke, horny, and salty.

For the second time, I added up my bills for the month.

"Damn! Not including my tuition, I need an extra twenty-two hundred dollars a month." I mumbled to myself.

I recalculated as if the figures might change. But the money I needed didn't include anything else that Brian's lavish taste might desire. So far, there had been nothing uplifting about being with this married man. Actually, this encounter had added unnecessary stress that I didn't need in my life. On top of everything else, I needed a way to make some quick cash fast.

"Lil Mia Latham . . ." the husky Grenadian voice announced.

I held up my head to see who knew me well enough to refer to me as *little Mia*. Bringing back some of my childhood memories, I remembered him instantly.

"Hi." I said greeting him with my warm but exhausting smile.

David Foster, my next door neighbor for practically all of my childhood, reached across the horseshoe counter and hugged me tight. I hadn't seen him in ten years, but this fifty-six-year-old man looked to be in his early forties which let me know that life had been treating him well.

I was taken back to the time when women would pass through his house like trains passing through Grand Central Station, despite the fact that he had a wife. Now that I'm old enough to appreciate the finer things in life, I understand why he was my first crush.

"I have to say, you have turned into such a beautiful woman."

I blushed at his smooth compliment.

"Thank you, and from what I can remember, you haven't changed a bit either."

David looked down at himself as if he forgot what he looked like. For an older man, he kept himself in good shape. He chose a pair of jeans and a white-button down as his casual look for the day. David took his hand and smoothed out his lightly mixed goatee. He winked his almond shape eye at me, giving me the same fluttering heart as he did years ago.

"Thanks. How old are you now . . . eighteen . . . nineteen?"

"Actually I'm twenty. I'll be twenty-one in a week."

"Is that so . . . well I'm going to have to take you to dinner to celebrate. And we can catch up on old times." he suggested.

"That sounds nice. Is your wife coming?" I asked.

David laughed showing off his perfect recapped teeth.

"No, Gloria won't be joining us."

I didn't really care whether or not she was in the picture. In this situation, I just needed to know how much wiggle room I had. I could tell by the way that he looked at me that he wanted more than just general conversation and dinner.

"You're looking more and more like your mother." he added in approval.

"I hope that's a good thing."

"It certainly is." he whispered seductively.

The door to the dental office buzzed when somebody came in. My eyes widened with surprise as Brian walked authoritatively towards us.

"I need you to come with me." he said with an attitude.

"Excuse me for a second."

Brian was walking so close to me that he was stepping on the heels of my shoes. Once I got to a vacant exam room Brian stepped in behind me, and I shut the door.

"So this is what you gonna' do?" he asked.

"What are you talking about? Do what?" I asked confused.

"You sneak behind my back flirting and acting like a common whore. How long have you been sleeping with him? He ain't up in your face for no reason . . ." he continued.

"Who Brian? Oh, you talking about David . . ." I laughed. "He's my next door neighbor from when I was a little girl."

"Well you ain't a little girl no more. I seen how much lust he had in his eyes for you."

"Oh please Brian. It's not like that." I said flagging him off along with his false accusations.

He grabbed hold of my arm forcefully. I tried to pull away from him, but his grip got tighter confusing me even more. It was okay for him to do him, but when he thought that one of his women was going to get away, it was a problem.

"Are you serious? Let me go Brian you're hurting me." I whispered so that no one would hear us.

"Don't get yourself hurt because you wanna be a slut." he said. "I came here to get three hundred dollars."

He let go of my arm, and I rubbed it.

"I don't have any more money. I used it all on your truck and I don't get paid until tomorrow."

"That's old shit that I don't wanna hear about again. I knew that this was a mistake. That's exactly what I get for slumming."

Brian's words and actions pierced my brain and caused it to ache. Everything was moving so fast, but not fast enough for common sense to have a chance to kick in sooner. Brian was using me, and I didn't get a chance to benefit from what we were doing. I had to keep him around long enough to get what I needed out of this arrangement. I couldn't lose out again.

"Wait here."

I left him alone and stood outside of the door. I heard the voices of Dr. Lyons and Celia in with a patient. I'd been working here so long that I knew the ins and outs. This time the sound of the drill pinched my nerves as I went into the doctor's private office. Looking around nervously, I opened his desk drawer. The petty cash wasn't meant to support my habit, but I had no other choice in the matter. The dental practice could recover from this loss, but I couldn't if I let Brian get away over something as minor as money.

I placed the money into a file that sat on the edge of the cluttered desk and walked out of the office. When I handed it to him, he counted it. Brian didn't say another word as he left the office with stolen money. David got up from his seat.

"Is everything okay?" he asked.

I never took my eyes off of Brian.

"Yes." I said trying to forget what just happened.

"Good, now what time should I pick you up for dinner?"

6

The celebration of the day I came into this world was turning out to be a miserable one for me. Here it is: I turned twenty-one today and was stood up by Brian. Earlier, he stopped by to get the money for his rims. He threw me a quickie and ran off to frivolously spend money that I didn't have but gave so freely.

Why does anything Brian do continue to surprise me? The only things he'd been giving me during the last four months were the male parts that I could get from any man. Let me not speak too soon. I don't think its gets any better than what Brian was blessed with. But I couldn't hang my hopes on the uncertainty that he may or may not come back, so I had to do the next best thing.

David impressed me when I climbed into his 1960 fire-red Mustang. He shut the door behind me like a true gentleman. I took this brief opportunity to check him out. Um, I thought that Brian was the only one that could make me feel this way. I guess not because David was looking sexy in his tailored black suit and salmon shirt that showed his gold lighting blot pendant. Before he got back into the car, I checked my phone to see if Brian was going to go against the odds and keep his promise to make my 21st birthday memorable. He lied again. I turned my phone off and gave myself to the man that actually had time for me.

The conversation alone had me feeling secure with my decision to take this other married man up on his offer for dinner. This wasn't just any random married man. I was too close to this situation. He knew my parents, and his wife used to baby-sit me. Now, I'm keeping her husband company. I'm sorry for her, but its not like I initiated the situation . . . I just took him up on an offer that I couldn't refuse at a vulnerable time.

Infiniti Lounge was tucked away in midtown, Myrtle Beach. I assumed he chose this location so we wouldn't run into any nosy-ass gossipers in Georgia. Whatever the reasons were for coming so far away, it didn't matter to me. Anything was better than sitting home alone, especially today.

"You look so beautiful tonight." he said for the eighth time since we sat down.

My eyes focused on the mandarin-strapless dress instead of making direct-eye contact with him. I was hearing and appreciating his chivalry, but it was coming from the wrong person. Instead of enjoying this meal and good company, I was worried about what Brian was doing and who he was doing it to? I drew in a breath of smoky air and continued to play with the Salmon salad that sat on the end of my fork.

"I'm going to be honest David. I'm curious, why me? I mean I remember vividly the many women in your life. Sneaking out the back door when your wife was coming in the front door . . ."

"Wow, you remember that . . ."

"Yes I do. That's why I wanna know, are you just trying to add me to your count?" I asked wanting to be clear on where we stood. "I'm just not another dumb-young booty that you can feed, fuck and forget." I spoke honestly.

David laughed before he swallowed the rest of his Jack Daniels and Coke. I expected for him to tell me what he thought I wanted to hear, but I needed him to say something so that I could numb my heart against any bullshit that he might throw my way. I was already in one mess that I was trying to get out of, I didn't need anymore unnecessary problems.

"Baby girl, you answered your own question. I'm not lacking in the women department. I'm not going to sit here and lie and tell you that I'm not attracted to you, because I am. I got to restrain myself just from being all over you. We can take things at your pace and see where things go."

David waived his hand in the air. I didn't know what that was about until I saw two waitresses come towards the table with multiple bags. The last one was carrying a small butter crème cake. He moved our dinner plates aside, and she sat the cake in front of me. I was speechless and wrong.

"I didn't know what to get you, so I got you everything that reminded me of you. Go ahead and make a wish and blow out your candles."

I think part of my wish had finally come true. Surrounded by the bags signed with designer names, I was feeling guilty for accusing him of having a motive. I guess that I was planting my bad seed in his backyard when he was being nothing but genuine.

"I need to apologize to you."

"For what?" he asked.

"For doubting you. Sometimes I think that people have good intentions for me, but then they turn out to be selfish assholes. That's why I asked you that question."

"Well, you don't have nothing to worry about. You have me to look out for you now. And I promise, I won't let anyone hurt you. Turn around and close your eyes. I have something else for you." he said sincerely.

I did what he said. Surprisingly, a cold symbol touched my bare skin. David placed a fourteen-karat-gold-fire-and-ice necklace around my neck.

"I can't take this, this is too expensive . . ." I said falsely looking into the mirror that I fished from the bottom of my multi-colored bag.

"It is, but you can and you will. Happy Birthday, baby!" he said kissing me on my lips and I didn't resist.

Emotional about what David had showed me this evening, I fought back the tears that I had bottled up in me for different reasons. I bet he thought that I was falling for him, but these were tears of happiness because he was going to give me everything I needed to compete with Solae and to keep Brian around a little while longer. Everything was finally falling into place. This birthday wasn't so bad after all.

The multiple light taps woke me out of a peaceful sleep. When I initially opened my eyes I didn't remember where I was at first.

"Good morning, sweetie."

And then I remembered.

David leaned in to kiss me, but I turned my head. He was getting too close for my comfort. I had to admit that for a man his age, his sex game ranked in the top-five on my list. Now, that the dust had settled, I had to accept the fact that David pleasured me into the early morning hours instead of Brian. I was over the high and more than ready to go find Brian. But with all my feelings about what had been going down in my life, I wasn't stupid enough to lead David to believe that I didn't want him. I just wanted what he had to offer, but my actions were going to come across the same.

"What's wrong did I do something?"

"No, its just that I haven't been in the bathroom yet." I managed.

"Oh, I understand. How about we go and get some breakfast. After that, I can take you to this little boutique that I think that you are gonna' love."

"David, you don't have to do that. You already did enough . . ."

"Please, money is not a problem if that's what you're worried about. I'm falling in love with you, so there isn't anything that I wouldn't do for you. So stop fighting me Mia and let me show you how you deserve to be treated."

I propped up on my elbows. David was taking this too far. I wasn't the little girl that he knew years ago. I was grown now and interested in different things. I required more than an ice cream cone from the store. And although David was showing me the difference between men and boys, talk was cheap. He needed to prove his words true in order for me to believe them.

"I like you, but using the word love is taking it a little too far. Besides, what would Gloria say?"

"I need to tell you something."

I eased out of the bed taking the sheet with me.

"What is it? Tell me . . ." I said in a panic with crazy thoughts cascading through my mind.

"Oh, no its nothing like that. That day at the office when you went to the back, I looked at your notebook. I see that you need help and I can give it to you."

My heart slowed down when I realized that it wasn't something serious for me to worry about. But I still felt some type of way that he was up in my business when I didn't invite him in.

"Yeah, I'm having a little money problem. But who isn't?"

"Listen, what I say to you never leaves this room." he said.

"Okay." I responded, leaning in close to hear how he was going to solve my problem.

"You work at a dentist's office?"

I shook my head.

"You get a hold of a prescription pad. We are going to write prescriptions for drugs in aliases for: Codeine, Oxycontin, Perks, Xanax, and Valium . . . I have this friend that works in an Alabama pharmacy. He agreed to fill the scripts. We give him a little bit for his troubles, and we sell on the street, split the profits and . . ."

"I don't know, what if we get caught, or I get fired. Hell, I ain't going to jail! I'm not built for that life!" I said shaking my head.

"That won't happen unless you start running your mouth." he said.

"I don't know David . . ."

"You must like being broke. Don't say I didn't try to help you."

David sat on the side of the bed in a towel reaching for the remote control. He let my rejection fade into thin air. Come to think about it, I never knew how he made his money to keep him in the upper-middle class lifestyle that kept him more than comfortable.

I thought about Brian's needs and that made me consider selling drugs. It wasn't like I was hurting anybody. It would be easy money to help me to get out of the red and then I would be done. The root of all evil, in my opinion, wasn't money. It was men because they had me doing shit I would never dream of doing until I met them.

"How much are we talking?" I interrupted his gaze at the basketball game.

"We can clear a grand a week, I already have people waiting on orders."

"I'm in."

7

What I was doing had become as effortless as breathing. I sat on the sofa with the dictionary in my lap. It was turned to where I put the blank prescriptions. I wasn't worried about getting caught because my boss was old and showing signs of dementia. If he got curious as to where the missing prescription pads were, all I had to do was convince him that he must have misplaced them. It was just that easy.

To avoid suspicion, I wrote five prescriptions and faxed them to David's connection in Alabama from the free library. I didn't mind taking that long drive because David was making it worth my while.

I acted like I had been living this life for a long time because I was fearless and confident with what I was doing. As soon as I got out of the rental car this nervous guy, pacing the parking lot behind Emerson's Pharmacy, looked over his shoulder.

"Who are you? I was expecting D." he said.

"Don't worry about that. I'm here and the same rules still apply." I said.

This was my tenth deal in a month. I was okay with doing it alone because David had prearranged everything before hand, so I knew what I was walking into. I didn't realize how seedy people really were until I got hooked up with David. Although he had his softer-side, I would hate to be on his bad-side now that I knew what kind of company he kept.

"This can be a setup. I don't know you." he insisted.

I put my hands on my hips, showing my growing annoyance. His hesitation was causing me to lose money. I don't know what possessed David to do business with this nervous man. Just by being around him for a minute, I could tell that if anything went down he would snitch on us at the drop of a dime. He pushed his thick-rimmed glasses on his long, wide nose. Although there was no sun out, he wiped beads of sweat from his honey-colored forehead. His fidgeting upset his stripped shirt revealing the handle of a gun. I held my stance to avoid tearing out of his parking lot forgetting what I came here for.

"Boy, I ain't got no time or patience to be setting no one up, especially you. Give me what I came here for, so I can pass off and go about my business."

"It's all there." he stuttered.

I took the bag making sure that everything was inside that was suppose to be. When I was satisfied, I gave him the money and left.

The long drive allowed me to clear my mind. I considered my benefactor's feelings by me stringing the two of them along. But quickly decided to keep them both. I didn't see where they were concerned with my feelings to the point that they would sacrifice anything for my happiness. Oh, well I had to do what was beneficial to me.

When I got home, all that was on my mind was a hot bath, Chinese food and my warm bed. I pulled up to my front door, and knew my plans had just changed. It was 11:43 p.m., and David was sitting on my front step, unannounced.

"I wasn't expecting you until tomorrow."

"I know but I needed to be with you tonight." he said.

"What's wrong?"

I rubbed his cheek the way he liked.

"Lets go inside and we'll talk."

My heart was racing because of the unknown. I could barely open the door because my hands were shaking so badly from what I assumed he needed to say. I didn't have a backup plan for just incase. I wasn't worried about if he left me or not, I just didn't want to lose the extra income.

"Okay, what's wrong David? You're scaring me again." I said.

The possibility of someone finding out what we had been doing scared the hell out of me.

"Relax sweetie. Its nothing like that. I just love being around you, and I wanna make you happy. First things first, I got your money from last week."

I smiled because this is what I was waiting for. I opened the envelope.

"All of this?" I asked.

"Yes, twenty-two hundred-and-forty dollars. I told you that I would look out for you," he responded. "And I got us some Chinese food and this is for you."

He smiled proudly at his rewards for me.

When he was at my door unexpectedly, I overlooked the bags that were in his hands. I was happy with the cash, but everything else was extra. And I deserved it. I sat down on the bench in the foyer and took my gifts.

"David are you serious?" I asked examining the diamond teardrop earrings.

"Yes, I want you to have them. Oh, one more thing. Are you busy on the 12th?"

"I doubt it. Wassup?"

"I'm going to New York, so I want you to come with me."

"Okay."

"There's something else." he said seriously.

I braced myself as much as I could. His frequent over-exaggerated surprises were getting to be annoying. He grabbed my hand, kneeling at my feet. I shook my head no. I hoped he wasn't doing what I think he was doing.

"Wait, before you start. I can't marry you."

He laughed non-stop, while I dissected the meaning of all the laughter.

"What?" I asked.

"Honey, I wasn't going to ask you to marry me. I was going to tell you that I left my wife." he said with no emotion.

My mouth hung open in shock. This was almost as bad as him proposing to me. I wasn't feeling his decision because I didn't want a full commitment, and he knew that. I hoped that by leaving his wife, he wasn't trying to trick or force me into something that I didn't want. After all that had happened to me, I feel like it is easier to cope without being confined to a relationship. Besides, what could David possibly give me in a relationship that he wasn't giving me now?

"Why would you go and do a thing like that?" I asked.

"Because I found the one I want to spend the rest of my life with. Yeah, after twenty-seven years of marriage I left my wife for you Mia." he said letting the reality sink in.

8

"Mia, I need to talk to you."

Solae didn't wait for me to invite her inside. She stepped into the living room and fell back onto the loveseat. I stood at the door holding my robe together although it was already tied. My head was outside the door, and I looked up and down the street as the mild winter's wind dried the forming sweat on my head. My heart was racing because it seemed that as soon as Brian had shut the door, there was a knock. This was a little too close for comfort, but it wasn't enough for me to end it with him. I shut the door and sat across from her.

"I can see I'm interrupting something." she said.

This was nerve-wracking, because I could tell that Solae had been crying. She never cried over anything as long as I'd known her, so I knew that this must have been deep.

"Is Jeremy here? Tell him I said hi." she continued through a few sniffles not coming straight to the point.

"No, its just me and you."

"Oh."

She wiped her nose.

"What is that smell?" she inquired.

I sniffed the air, playing off the fact that my apartment smelled like sex and Brian's oil.

"Nothing girl, you imagining things. Wassup, why are you crying?" I asked.

"I think Brian is cheating on me."

I broke out in laughter. This was the craziest thing that I had heard in a long time. How could a married man cheat on his mistress when he was cheating on his wife with her.

"Did I say something funny?"

"Yes, did you hear what you just said. Your married lover is cheating on you . . ."

When a woman's intuition is screaming that there's deception, there usually is. If she thought that those tears were going to get sympathy from me, then she had another thing coming. As far as I was concerned, karma was just knocking at her door. Whether or not she welcomed it, it wasn't going anywhere.

Now that I knew what she had come here for and that she was full of shit as usual, I sat back on my sofa hugging my blueberry pillow. My focus turned towards possible decorating ideas because I wasn't interested in discussing Brian, especially with her.

"This is my life we're talking about, so there ain't a damn thing funny. I gave this dude my heart and risked my marriage only to have him cheat on me! I will kill that nigga and the bitch when I find out who she is!" she yelled standing over me as if she sensed it was me without realizing it. It's ironic how people can give it out but can't take it.

"You need to calm down. Ain't no man worth going to jail over. And you have to put yourself in her shoes. Who says that Brian told her about you?"

I gave her food for thought. By the way she turned her face up, I could tell that Solae wasn't digesting this change of events.

"What, you know who this bitch is? Cause you sure as hell taking up for her."

"Solae you know I love you, but right now you talking crazy! I don't know nothing except for what you're telling me."

She fell to the floor laying in my lap sobbing. I had never seen her like this before, a hot mess. Finally, I was on top while she was crumbling at my pedicured feet. I knew that I shouldn't gloat over her misery, but she was finally living my life. I wondered how she was going to feel when she found out that the least likely person took her man away from right under her nose. She really don't have anyone to blame but herself. As I remember clearly, she forced him on me.

"I must be going crazy because you are even starting to smell like him."

Solae's drama was too much for me to deal with. I just didn't have time for her. This was my season, and I wasn't going to make it about her. I needed to give Brian a heads up as soon as I got rid of the whiny-ass chick who was getting on my damn nerves.

"You need to go home and get some rest," I told her subtly leading her to the door. "I got to go to work, but once I'm done I'm going to call and check on you."

I didn't give her a chance to respond, I shut the door.

The phone rang once. I fell onto the bed subconsciously gloating over what had just happened.

"Hello." she whispered.

"Who's this?" I asked.

"Who do you want to speak with?"

"Brain, but you didn't answer my question, who are you?" I asked with obvious agitation.

"I'm his friend and that's all you need to know." she responded nonchalantly.

"Well, I'm his girlfriend." I told her.

"Um, I doubt that." she snickered.

"Just put Brian on the phone!"

There was a light conversation in the background, and the phone went dead. I held it away from my face. How quickly had the tables turned. And who in the hell did he think he was having another bitch answer his phone? I wasn't going to waste anytime stressing and crying like Solae was earlier. I was going over there.

I wasn't interested in the formal pleasantries of the front desk clerk. I knew exactly where I was going, but when I got there, I didn't know what I was going to do or if I was going to make things worst than what they were already.

"Brian, come the fuck out here with that bitch!" I yelled banging on the door.

I'm not sure what was happening to me. I was so mad that I felt like my head was going to explode. My heavy body was sweaty, and I couldn't gather any sane thought. I just needed Brian to feel what I was feeling, but I knew that this was wishful thinking because it was obvious that I was disposable.

My fist was aching from banging even harder. Who did he think he was? These females had him feeling himself. He actually thought that he could be disrespectful, and that I'd be okay with that insanity. I put my ear up to the door because this nigga was pretending like he wasn't in there with his side-piece. I paused and didn't take into consideration that my best friend could have been in there with my man before I started acting a fool. If Solae was in there, she was going to find out who had been keeping him away from her.

Tired and stressed, my back rested against 813 when I kicked the door, rattling the entire foundation. I blocked out the nosy neighbors that stuck their heads outside their door to see what was going on.

"I think you need to leave now!" he warned me from behind the door.

Brian wasn't shit, plain and simple. It wasn't that he wasn't capable of fixing things with me. Brian didn't want to and that was pissing me off.

"Come out here and face me like a man! Come . . . . Out . . . Here . . . Brian . . . !" I yelled in repetition with the kicks to his door.

"Just go home! I told you before that we will never be together! I don't know how else to tell you. Stop stalking me, and just go!" he raised his voice a little louder.

I replayed our affair over in my head: We had sex, he took my gifts, he played mind games, cheated on me, fit me in his life when it was convenient for him, but never had he even uttered a single word that *it was over*. And now that he had announced to everybody that I was *stalking him*, he had to pay for that lie.

"That's fine. You wanna pretend that you don't know me? I'm going to tell your wife and congregation everything that has been going on! And trust me Brian, I have the messages to prove that I'm not crazy!"

The elevator door opened, and two sheriffs stepped off. I laughed shaking my head at what he just did. The door opened behind me.

"Sir, did you report a disturbance?" she asked Brian.

"I did . . ." he said.

"Who is she to you?"

Brian hesitated, and rubbed his hands over his face before he spoke. I said nothing.

"A lost sheep that I tried to minister to. It's obvious that she has some real deep-rooted issues. Look at my door," he pointed. "I guess she misread the signs of my guidance for something more." he said putting on his minister's face.

"Do you want to press charges?" she asked anticipating another notch on her belt.

I waited for his answer.

"Yes I do." Brian said boldly without hesitation.

"Miss turn around and place your hands behind your back."

This was a fuckin' nightmare. When I get out of jail, his life was going to be hell, compliments of me, *his stalker*.

This was an omen of what my life would be like if I continued to deal with this married minister. I wasn't a very religious person, but it didn't take much for me to realize that I was breaking some serious commandments. *God* was punishing me for my poor choices and he let me know by allowing me to get thrown in jail. I used to think that Brian was worth it, until he showed me that I meant nothing to him. If I went back to him on a fluke, I'd be getting everything I deserved.

What made me snap back into this nightmare was the sobs of the middle-aged woman sitting next to me. She seemed to be normal, pretty, and nicely dressed. I couldn't envision what could have brought her to a miserable place like jail. I bit my tongue for as long as I could.

"Are you okay?"

Between her heavy flow of tears, she mumbled.

"My life is over."

"No it's not." I replied.

"I killed somebody tonight."

She dabbed her eyes with the sleeve of her torn-wrinkled-crimson shirt. What immediately came to mind was that I didn't belong here, and her issue confirmed that for me. Now that I knew what she was capable of, I wanted to end the conversation quickly. Instead, I moved as far away from her as I could before I continued.

"Wow, I'm sorry." I said in a hardly recognizable voice.

"Well, I'm not. I been with that bitch Lea for thirteen years. I sacrificed a lot for her and lost even more because of my lifestyle. And that bitch had the nerve to leave me for a woman half-her age. Shit! I was the one that should have walked out on her broke, abusive ass years ago. But no, I thought that things would change. I had hopes that she would get better if I did what she wanted me to do. Yeah, it got real when I ran her ass over tonight," she said in a bone-chilling tone. "A life for a life. Now that bitch'll be sleeping with the devil." she ended.

The hairs on the back of my neck stood up. This was another eerie glimpse into my future if I kept compulsively chasing a man that wasn't worth the effort. I was done. I knew who my one phone call was going to be to so I waived the CO over to me.

"Can I make my phone call now?" I asked.

He shook his head.

"Good luck sis." she said as I got up.

"No, good luck to you." I said walking away from that depressing situation.

"Hey David, its Mia. I need a huge favor." I said holding the payphone away from my ear. "I'm at Fulton County PD. Can you come and get me?"

"Did they find it?" he asked.

It processed after a minute.

"No, I had some parking tickets. They got me for that." I lied to him for the second time.

He let out a hard breath.

"I'm on my way." he said without hesitation.

9

I never told David the truth about why I was in jail, and he never asked me. He also never asked for the five-hundred dollars back that he used for my bail. Remembering the things that Brian had said the other day hurt beyond mere comprehension. The fact that he painted the illusion that I was some crazy stalker made it hard for me to put everything behind me. But I had to, because I knew better than anyone that, he wasn't sitting around regretting anything that he'd done to me. Besides, the restraining order that he has out on me, made us officially done.

My head rested on David's bare chest as I listened to the beats of his heart that coincided with the consistent ticks of the clock. My new found comfort zone had me questioning everything that I initially thought. In the beginning of our relationship, I was having a major problem adjusting to the fact that he wasn't Brian. But now in hindsight, dealing with David is actually better than being stressed out, being thrown in jail and constantly worrying about where he was laying his *roots*. There is no question in my mind about David because my bed is never cold at night and I know that he will never leave me.

"What are you thinking about?" he asked placing a soft kiss on my forehead.

"Nothing in particular." I responded faintly.

"I'm not so sure about that because that *nothing*, kept you up most of the night tossing and turning."

It scared me how much David knew the real me. Every time that I was around him I tried unsuccessfully to mask my pain of what Brian did to me. And this time like every other, he read me like an open book.

"Actually, I thought that me selling drugs was going to bring me some real money . . ." I said revealing part of my issue.

"Wait, let me stop you right there. What we do isn't *selling drugs*. You make it sound so dirty. Educate yourself on the terms of this business," he scolded like I was one of his eight children. "We provide black market pharmacuticles to the medically dependent." he schooled me.

I think that David forgot who he was talking to. He could put a fancy tuxedo on the lie if that's what he chose to do. But I was keeping our situation a hundred percent honest.

I sucked my teeth.

"I want more money!" I whined.

"Be careful what you put out into the atmosphere." he told me.

"I'm serious babe, I want more money and I don't care how I get it. Now that you got me accustomed to a certain lifestyle, it got good to me. I should be in another tax bracket by now and living like that as well," I pouted. "I'm tired of faking a good-life still shopping at Target . . . I deserve Bloomingdales." I ranted.

"Babe, its not been that long and you alone cleared seven grand. And what have you been doing with your money anyway?" he asked. "What more do you want?"

"Money, haven't you been listening to anything that I've been saying? And what I do with my money is my business. I earned it, so please don't question me."

"I got you."

David started kissing me letting me know that he was ready for the second time this morning. I can see how much he enjoyed *me*, so if I needed to use this as my secret weapon . . . I would.

"Don't touch me. If you ain't trynna' provide for me, then you won't be getting none of this for a very long time." I said teasing him with my naked body.

"When have I ever promised you anything and haven't come through? Never, I'm a man of my word and I'm going to get you more money. What are you willing to do to change your bracket?"

Without hesitation I responded knowing that this old soul always had a lucrative hustle.

"What do you have in mind?"

"I got this guy in New York. I need to get him some product. That's where you come in at. I need you to put it on you."

"So that's what this trip is about today. And what do you mean put it on me? Why can't you do it?" I said pacing the floor.

"Because you have a face that no one will ever suspect of smuggling."

"I gotta' draw the line somewhere. What if I get caught? I can't go back to jail. It was horrible in there."

"Well, I suggest you don't get caught. Besides, I can remember you telling me that you would do anything to get money."

David's true colors were showing, and they were ugly shades of grey and black. He didn't care if I got caught and went back to jail. He was just concerned about making money. I was all for that plan until I became the main source.

"I guess you already had your answer before you brought this to me."

"I just figured since I did all I did for you, including leaving my wife for you, that you could do this one small thing for me." he said. "You said that you'll do anything for more money. I told you to be careful what you put out into the atmosphere. I held true to my word, so hold true to yours. Besides, we both will benefit from this transaction."

He reached beside the bed and started peeling off on the wrinkled covers.

"To show you how I do, here's two stacks up front."

I hated nothing more than for someone taking care of me voluntarily and then throwing it back in my face. This was his attempt to guilt me into doing something that I wouldn't want to do otherwise. I never had a gun to his head telling him to do any of that for me. I rolled my eyes and took the money.

"If we're gonna' do this, then we need to get ready." I backed down without a fight.

When I was sure JFK Airport was out of view, I let out my breath. It felt like I didn't breath for the entire flight because I was sure I was going to get caught. Two things I now knew for sure: I got away with it, and I was never going to do this again. I put on my sunglasses to hide the forming tears in my eyes.

"Oh, so you're gonna' sit there and give me the silent treatment?" David asked already knowing the answer since I hadn't said a single word to him in five miles.

The primary reason for my quietness was because I couldn't speak, even if I wanted to. The fear of what I had done was weighing heavy on me. I was *willing* to do anything for him, especially since he'd been so good to me and I didn't want the good life to end. But even though I made it to New York without incident, I still felt used by David.

"I really don't have nothing to say."

"Babe, you'll be fine. I'm not sure what you're used to, but I will never do anything to hurt you or get you in trouble."

I relaxed instantly because I believed him because that's all he'd shown me. And since I did this for him, I was going to burn a hole in his pockets.

Fifteen minutes from the Bronx Expressway, we pulled up to an apartment building on Sedgewick Avenue. I knew how David operated, so I got relaxed in the seat. I knew that this exchange wasn't going to be too long.

"I want you to come in with me." he said turning off the ignition.

"I really don't feel like it."

"Please for me? I wanna show my baby off."

Damn, this was an extreme change for me. I went from one man keeping me in his secret closet to another man that wouldn't let me alone. I just wanted to get it over with so I could shop and go back home.

I sat on a kitchen chair that they used as living room furniture. My entire body was held together because I was scared to move. With all the clutter around me, I wasn't sure what my jump out. There were two kids sitting in front of the massive television and playing *Xbox*. Nothing matched in this crayon box sized room. And the bright orange walls started to give me a migraine. I forced the distasteful look off of my face when a female in her mid-twenties sat on a crate by my chair. She was staring at me until I turned and gave her a nervous smile.

"Hi." I said.

"My husband thinks you cute." she said.

I didn't know how to respond to that comment; that subject was a tricky one to touch, so I decided to leave it alone.

"You know, I don't mind my man seeing other women 'cause I know he's coming home to his family at the end of the night."

She was giving up unsolicited information which left me questioning women in general. Do we put up with all the shit that we do just because we can say that we have a man? I felt sorry for her because I used to be there.

"And that's all that matters." I responded.

"So how do you feel about Quentin?"

"I don't feel nothing. I don't know him."

"Well, I can arrange that."

I looked right through her maple exterior. She had the lowest self-esteem that I'd ever seen, and it quickly made me sad. Was this how I acted with Brian? Although I wasn't offering him out to other women just to please him, I still settled for his bullshit and disrespect. The concept was one in the same. So before I told her to go to hell with her bullshit request, David came out of the kitchen with Quentin.

The short, chestnut-brown, handsome guy, standing next to David, was half of David's age. I turned my head to keep him from staring because I felt every eye in the room on me.

"Love, I have to talk to you for a second."

I got up and followed him out into the hallway.

"What's wrong now?"

"What lengths would you go to make me happy?" he asked sounding like Brian.

"Where is all of this coming from?" I asked.

"I'm just asking. Would you do anything to make me happy like I make you happy?"

"Yes I would." I spoke prematurely.

"I always had this fantasy . . ." he spoke. "I always wanted my woman to have sex with another man while I watched."

David's lips were moving, but nothing coming out of it was making any sense to me.

"My wife wasn't with that no matter what I gave her. And Quentin is really interested in you."

"You got to be fucking kidding me. I'm not a hoe. You can't pass me around for your pleasure. And how would you view me after that happen? You're crazy to even suggest that."

"I won't look at you differently. It's just my fantasy, but I guess you don't love me like I thought. Maybe I left my wife for nothing."

He had the nerve to stand in my face doubting my loyalty to him. He was the one approaching me with his thoughtless, self-gratifying fantasy that benefited only him and Quentin. And he was doubting me.

"Don't do that shit to me. I never asked for anything or for you to leave your damn wife, so don't guilt me into doing what I don't want to do."

"You just don't love me, and now I know. I won't waste anymore of my time on you so find your way home. And give me my damn jewelry back!"

He said snatching my necklace off of my neck. I held my chest where he left it bare.

"Are you kidding me David? Did you just do that? You gonna' leave me in New York to?" I said shocked by his actions.

"Sure as a heart-attack. Bye!" he said pushing me away from him.

I can't believe that this was happening and to me, let alone from David. This demand left me broken. I didn't care how he felt. He could keep the damn necklace, but he wasn't leaving me in this neighborhood alone.

"Unless . . . never mind . . ."

"Say it. You said everything else today."

"Did I mention that I was willing to give you five-thousand dollars, and he's gonna' match that if you do this?"

"No you didn't mention that detail."

10

I refused David's offer to bring me home, especially since he put me in that awkward position back in New York. I climbed out of the cab with a dozen bags and ten-thousand dollars in cash tucked in a shoebox. I told myself that when I stepped foot in my own home, I would be erasing the entire experience. And that is what I intended on doing.

"Mia." the familiar voice glided out.

I spun around bringing back everything that I forced myself to forget.

"What are you doing here, Brian?"

"I needed to see you."

"I find that hard to believe, especially after you got me locked up."

"That's what I wanted to talk to you about."

"You said everything that you needed to that day. And you choosing to talk about what happened weeks later, isn't of any relevance at this point. Now I'm tired, and all I want to do is go to bed."

"Oh, you must be tired from running around town with that geriatric." he laughed.

"Oh you stalking me now? And what I do, and who I do it with is my business. FYI that geriatric takes better care of me than you ever did."

"You telling me that he lays it down better than me?" he asked shocked by my revelation.

"Yup." I said with a straight face.

"I find that hard to believe. You're just mad at me, and that's why you're lying."

"Believe what you want to believe."

"*I'm sorry* . . . that's what I came here to say."

The wind was knocked out of my tired body. I couldn't believe *I'm sorry* came out of the mouth of the most selfish man I knew. This was the Brian that I'd been waiting to get to know for a long time. I was mad that it took all of that drama for him to realize that he was wrong for what he did to me. Without any hesitation, I accepted his apology and applied it to everything he put me through.

I watched silently as he turned and walked away from my door. I dropped my bags and went back outside.

"Would you like to come in for a cappuccino or something?"

"I'll come in for that... *or something.*"

I knew exactly what his lingo meant.

Tonight Brian didn't make up any lies for *having* to leave. I pinched myself because he was still here and in my bed. Just this gesture alone had me willing to put aside the fact that he had me locked up. Brian also told me that he was going to drop the pending charges that he had against me on Monday. He was really starting to see my side of things.

I ignored the door completely. I turned over in my bed cuddling up under Brian. I felt safe in his arms, until the knocking forced me to leave my man in bed alone. I was glad that Brian was a heavy sleeper. If he had not been, whoever was knocking at the door might have messed up what we had just fixed. The knocks got louder.

"Yes . . ." I said showing off my nighty.

Standing at my door was a woman with pain in her hazel eyes. She said nothing, but continued eyeing me from head to toe, making mental notes on my body. This scared me while trying to piece together her identity.

"Now I got an up-close look into the eyes of the devil that tempted my husband to walk away from his family after twenty-seven years."

"Excuse me? Who's your husband? And if he left you, I see why cause you don't have no respect coming here at five in the morning."

"Bitch, you know David is my husband! I been following y'all for the past three weeks. I saw you flaunting your hot ass around town with my husband . . ."

I hunched my shoulders because I didn't care, and she couldn't make me care.

"Hasn't your momma taught you anything?" she asked in a tired voice.

I could tell that Gloria thought that she knew me from somewhere, but she couldn't put her finger on it. I was looking into the face of the woman who practically raised me. She was like my surrogate mother, in that sense, but other than that she was no blood of mine. I didn't have to feel any remorse for my choice. It is what it is.

Gloria stood off to the side, allowing the light from the street lamp to shine down on me. The fresh rain blew in my direction cooling me off despite what was going down. I didn't care what this old, sagging bitch had to say because she had touched on a sore subject.

"Don't talk about my mom. You know nothing about her."

Her eyes widened at the exact time she figured me out.

"Yeah, I know your mother all too well. I know that she birthed a slut. The apple don't fall too far from the tree, Mia Latham." she hissed with particles flying at me.

The Gloria that I knew a long-time ago was no more. Life or should I say her cheating husband had taken a toll and beat her down. It showed considerably on her dull, heavily-lined-caramel face. Now that she knew exactly who I was, I opened the door wide stepping into the line of fire. My mom wasn't here to defend herself, so I had to do it.

"Well you can't blame my mom for your husband getting tired of your old ass . . . look at you! Pathetic! And if you needed to blame someone for David walking out on you, you didn't need to leave your own backyard to do so!"

"Your mother thought that she could have my husband, and that didn't work . . . even with all of her tricks . . ."

"And I got him. Now what? Get over the fact that he left you for me. You know that this is real, and that's why you're at my door at this time of morning . . ."

"And he gave you my jewelry!" she shrieked.

The earrings were dangling from my ears when Gloria yanked them out. I was done talking because she took this too far. I swallowed hard trying to keep down my hatred for her. Her age had a lot to do with me holding back because if she was anyone else, I would have trashed her when she came to my door disrespectfully. I turned to walked away when she grabbed me by my hair, pulling me back outside. Gloria continued mumbling about me taking her husband while throwing wild punches. She jerked my body violently as if I was a rag doll. The wet cement came from under me and I fell to the ground where she kicked me in my ribs. All of her years of hurt came pouring out on me. In some ways, I was paying for the sins of my mother.

The flashing lights got closer when six cop cars pulled up in front of the complex. I stayed up long after the fight, replaying the early-morning's events over and over again. Gloria acted as if I had committed some sort of crime by sleeping with her husband. If I had to do it all over again just to spare her heartache, I wouldn't change a thing because it paid off for me financially.

I couldn't hide in the bathroom all afternoon. Now that I couldn't barely breath or move without the pain radiating throughout my body, I'm mad that I refused medical treatment. I checked my face one more time and came out like nothing ever happened. If by chance Brian noticed the bruising, how was I going to explain that? I was forming a lie . . . just incase.

"Babe, do you want me to fix you something to eat?" I asked Brian as he sat on the side of my bed fastening his *Movado*.

"No I'm good, I'll grab something on the way to work."

This was one time that I wasn't going to debate his rejection or complain about him not paying me any attention. I knew that he wasn't going to work. Now that he was focused on the message to meet him at the *Hilton* in an hour. He didn't notice the black eye after I concealed it with foundation. As for the deep cut on my lip, it was hardly noticeable after the plum lipstick hid the truth. I'm glad that he slept through my attack, but I'm irritated as hell that I let that fifty-year-old woman beat my ass the way she did. I guess I was sorry for what I did to her.

"What are your plans for the day?" he asked.

"Not too much of anything." I responded.

"Well call me later and maybe we can catch a movie." he said kissing me on the forehead heading out the door before I had a chance to respond.

I was okay with his sudden exit. I stood at the window with the curtains pulled back. Brian sped off, I grabbed my bag and was right behind him.

Gloria's tired ass was getting acquainted with her temporary living arrangement, jail. I intended on making an example out of her. If every woman handled things the way she did this morning, then the system would be filled with a lot of scorn women. I knew that she would be trying to call David to bail her out, so I kept him occupied and his phone in my possession. Under any other circumstances, I wouldn't have considered going back to his bed, especially after New York, but I felt justified after what happened between me and his wife.

"I love you so much Mia. I always want you to remember that." he announced.

That statement hit me right in my heart. This felt different. For some reason, I believed him, but I forced it out. My main motive for being here was for the purpose of getting more materialistic possessions out of my sugar daddy and having something else to hold over his soon-to-be ex-wife's head.

I straddled him in the same bed that he shared with her for decades.

"You need to divorce that bitch!" I said through strokes.

"I . . . will . . ." he said through moans of pleasure. "Oh shit!"

When David didn't say another word, and his body went limp, I opened my eyes.

"David, don't play with me! Are you serious! You fell asleep on me?"

I tapped his face, and he didn't respond. Holding my tender ribs, I slid off of him and stood at the side of the bed, looking down at him.

"David, this shit ain't funny!"

Darkness hung in the room like the Grim Reaper on death row. My heart broke because I just knew. My tears wouldn't stop soaking my shirt. He didn't move, so I put my head on his chest and heard nothing.

"He's dead . . ." I mumbled.

I reached for my clothes. After I put one foot into my jeans, I nervously fell onto the uncovered floor adding to the throbbing pain, unable to process the severity of the sudden change in my life. In my entire life, I had only seen one-dead body. Being in direct contact with this one gave me the creeps, so my main focus was getting out of there. They wasn't gonna' pin no murder on me, especially since his wife had an ax to grind. Damn, I should have gotten him to change his beneficiary. It was too late for should haves now.

I went to the dresser and took some jewelry that was owed to me. I went where I knew he kept the money and pills and shoved them into my bag. Before I left, I walked over to David for the last time. He looked like he was in a peaceful sleep. I bent over him and kissed him on his warm cheek. I knew deep down inside, I would never find another sugar daddy like him in this lifetime.

11

Confessions are suppose to be good for the soul. Once I opened Pandora's box, there would be no going back. Anyone in my current situation would have mixed feelings. I kept calculating the dates and shook my head. Things were much simpler when I had control of the situation. But now that the outcome was different, I had no idea what I was going to do. It hadn't been my intention to let things get to this point. But just like life, it happened.

I flirted with the fact that Brian's raw and blatant disrespect for women was going to cause me a lot more problems. Thinking about this did the opposite of easing my fears. I knew why I waited six-and-a-half weeks to do this. I knew exactly what I was up against, this was going to be the ultimate fight of my life.

My hands started to tremble as I dialed the last number. As it rang in my ear, there was no sign of him picking up. I took a deep breath and relaxed because maybe next time, I might actually get up the nerve to tell him.

I was more than ready to hang up when he spoke, giving off a bad vibe.

"Hello." he said.

"We need to talk." I mimicked Solae.

"Who's this?" Brian asked.

My body tensed up immediately when I realized that Brian wasn't going to make this call easy. I let out a nervous laugh, hoping that he wasn't serious. There was silence on the other end which made me regret that I hadn't approached this a different way.

"It's Mia . . ." I said playing his mind game.

"Oh," he said dryly.

Brian was obviously uninterested in hearing from me today. Nauseous about what I needed to say, I was regretting that he was going to be the father of my child with every second that went by.

"Pregnant." I blurted out with an attitude.

I was glad that no one was in the dental office at this time. Subconsciously, I had already mentally prepared myself for the drama and doubts that were going to erupt from my Gemini. I waited for his response.

"I'm pregnant." I said one more time for verification.

I was going to be someone's mother. That thought was scary as hell. I couldn't believe it myself, but it was bound to happen.

"Um, are you calling me to setup a date for the Christening?"

This Brian I was all too familiar with. But he had warned me, so I couldn't be too mad. He was keeping everything professional as if someone was listening in on our call. If they were, they were about to get an ear full.

"Don't play with me! Brian I'm pregnant and it's yours. I hope you heard me because it's a fact."

Before he even said anything, I knew what he was thinking. He was silent to the point that I thought that he'd hung up on me.

"Did you hear what I just said? I'm pregnant, Brian, and its yours."

"Bitch you got some nerve to call me with this bullshit!" he yelled. "Especially when you was sleeping around with that old wormy man. You gave it up to me willingly, so don't act like you were a virgin. God only knows whose baby that could be. But his name ain't Brian Abrams."

"I wasn't alone. So what does that say about you?"

"I have poor judgment." he shot back.

After all that he took from me, he was acting like I was trying to trap him. Honestly I wasn't expecting him to have a change of heart either.

"Well, get used to me because we have eighteen years to deal with each other. You're old enough to know to wrap it up." I shot back.

"Explain this to me. I've been with my wife for years and she has never been pregnant. Then I meet you, and after a few booty calls, you turn up pregnant. How is that possible?"

"I'm just lucky, I guess."

"Your smart-ass mouth is going to get you hurt. But I'm a fair man, and I listened to your lies. Now, you listen to me . . ."

"No, you listen to me. I only want to hear how much you gonna' pay me a month."

"I knew it. It's all about the money, but let me tell you one thing you-money-hungry bitch. I'm never leaving my wife. So that bastard you carrying is not mine, and I'll surely go to hell before I give you a damn dime of my hard earned money," he said through clenched teeth. "Let me take that back. The only money that I'm willing to give you is a hundred dollars for an abortion. If it's more, you go out and sell your ass to get the rest cause that's what you do right? Solae told me all about that incident in Miami . . . so, I know laying on your back for money isn't new to you. I can tell you this honey, it's not even good enough to trade for a meal. So take what you can get while I'm being nice."

"Where do you think that I would get an abortion for that cheap, if I decided to get one?"

"In Louisiana. My momma used to talk about this witch doctor who used to sell dinners and do abortions out of her house . . . ."

"You make me sick!"

What he told me the first night I met him was bad enough. But now that I was on the receiving end, he had the nerve to suggest that I go and get a homemade abortion and chicken a dinner from some-wannabe doctor. I wiped the tears from my eyes.

"I tried to help." he said in an informal way.

"Go to hell!"

"I guess I'll see you there." Brian ended.

The dial tone echoed in my ear. I put the receiver down and stared at it as if it was tainted. I didn't need this, especially not at work. My emotions were all over the place. I was sad, angry, hungry, and scared, all at the same time. Being a pastor, Brian should have been more than what he was being. And how can I forgive Solae for telling a total stranger that I had sex for money? One thing was for certain: Brian was going to regret the day he screwed me, got me knocked up, and disrespected me. As far as I was concerned, my foe was going to regret the day she put me out there as a prostitute.

"Yeah . . ." I shook my head. "Payback is a spiteful, disgusting, vindictive, son-of-a-bitch."

Without any real information on the man that got me pregnant, I wouldn't get any money. Brian wasn't going to give up anything willingly, and I believed every word that he said. I needed to find out everything I possibly could about Brian. The website came up, and I typed: 404-341-2208 and waited. *"Brian Anthony Abrams. 8 Runnemede Court. East Point, GA."* I read.

This could have been done the easy way, but Brian wanted to do things the hard way. Now, I had no choice but to inform his wife, Traci, of what her husband had been up to. If being pregnant was going to cost me, then we were going to share the expenses.

The soft blue notepad stayed under my hand, as I wrote down his life history. Without looking up, I reached for my phone.

You don't know me, but we have your husband, Brian, in common. We've been sleeping with each other for a long time. He told me all about you, y'all dull sex life, and how you wasn't satisfying him. I'm just letting you know he's leaving you to be with me.

I sent the message and sat back, waiting for her to respond. I had confidence that I could persuade him to see things my way, now that I forced his hand. If it was the last thing I did, he was going to be mine.

"I don't have time for this shit. Weak females like you come cheap, and just because you had my husband, doesn't mean it wasn't temporary," I read aloud. *"Brian is never going anywhere."*

Lmao. You don't know shit. Brian is coming with me because he loves me, not you. Just like last year's shoes, you're outdated. He wants something up to date. I warned you, stay the hell away from my man, bitch!

She didn't respond to my last text, so I assumed she wanted to settle this verbally or possibly physically. I was going to give her that opportunity real soon.

The phone rang. I took in a full breath and answered.

"Hello."

"Gurl, don't hello me. Where have you been?" Solae asked.

I was disappointed that it wasn't him. I hadn't spoken to her in weeks. I had too much on my mind to deal with this fraud and her drama. I was going to make this conversation as short as possible.

"Around." I continued with my-one-word answers.

"Anyway, Brian and I just got back from our weekend trip to Jamaica."

I shook my head as if she could see me. He wasn't shit, and that's why he stood me up on Saturday. And today, he's acting like he don't know me.

"We had so much fun," she gloated. "What have you been up to?" she continued.

"Being pregnant." I said, tapping on my baby father's information.

"What!" her voice echoed through the phone.

"Yeah, six-and-a-half weeks."

"Who's the father? Because I know that you haven't been dealing with Jeremy."

She didn't waste any time getting that out-in-the open. It wasn't really any of her business, so I was going to keep everything on a-need-to-know basis.

"You don't know him."

"Oh, as long as it ain't one of my dudes."

She laughed but little did she know that my child's father was the man she'd been seeing.

"Is there something you want to tell me?"

"Not that I know of." I responded.

"Oh," she said. "It just feels funny. Maybe it's nothing. Anyway, I'm happy that I'm finally going to be an auntie. We have to plan your baby shower soon. You need to give the father my number, so I can get his invite list." she rambled.

"Wait, you're moving too fast for me."

"Okay, but what's his name cause baby daddy isn't working for me."

"Who's name?" I asked annoyed by this conversation.

"The father."

"Damn! Why is my business that damn important to you?" I snapped.

"I'm going to let that slide. I know it's the hormones."

There was a long pause.

"If I find out that you crossed me in anyway . . ." she said in an menacing voice.

"Listen, I don't take kindly to threats Solae. I've been putting up with your shit for years, and I'm over it. If you want to be in my life without minding my business then you're welcome to stay. If not you can lose my number!" I snapped partially foaming at the mouth.

"Mia, you don't wanna go here with me."

"Then I suggest you stay the fuck outta' my business."

12

Yesterday was David's memorial service and I couldn't bring myself to go because his wife hated me with a passion. And to avoid an inevitable fight, I kept my distance. Sitting at home wasn't doing me any good because all I did was think about him, in between my mind flip-flopping back to Brian and his nonsense.

I was hoping that anything would put my mind at ease, but it did nothing but bring back the first time that he came back into my life. I needed to come to the realization that he was dead and I had to live life without him. I knew that David wouldn't have wanted me to sit around mourning him forever, so I was going to use what he taught me to survive.

I pulled up to the Medical Arts Building and got out. This was a long weekend that Dr. Lyons gave the staff once a month to regroup, so I knew that I could slip in, get what I needed and get out unnoticed. I had to meet up with one of my clients this afternoon.

Time would not allow me to go through the middleman. Our supply of narcotics just came in a few days ago that I didn't log-in, so I decided to take some samples to fill my order. I stood in front of the cabinet contemplating whether or not this easy money was worth walking away from. If I stood here any longer,

I would have loss my nerve. I shoved the Codeine bottles into my bag and left the same way I came in.

One of the ultimate lessons that I've learned in this hustle was not to do dirt in my own neighborhood. Me and David never did business with this guy Riot before, so when he suggested to come to me, I quickly shut that request down. Because I would go almost anywhere for the price he was willing to pay, I went into his territory.

Belfield Projects was beneath me on every level, but the two-hundred and fifty dollars that he was paying for the *purple*, I took the slumming on the chin in order for my come-up. I stepped out of my car looking around for the white Caprice that Riot told me that he was going to be in. When he saw me walking towards the car he flashed his lights once and I shook my head in confirmation that I was who I said I was.

This giant of a man crawled out of the car breathing like a bull that had just run a marathon. I swallowed hard, as the sound of sneakers scrapped the basketball courts at the makeshift park across the street from where we were. With the sun in my eyes I tried to see his face clearly, but I couldn't make out the distorted figure.

"Do you have the stuff?" he asked.

"Yeah, for seven-fifty."

"No bitch, its free."

I wasn't understanding what he was talking about until he put the barrel of the gun directly in the center of my pale forehead. Without hesitation I handed everything over willingly.

"Get on the ground and put your hands behind your head and count to twenty." he said.

I kissed the ground he walked on with his size twelve boots.

"One, two, three . . . ." I said.

I heard the car start up and he was gone just as quickly as he came.

Last night I barely escaped with my life realizing that this life wasn't for me and David was obviously the brains behind our operation. Any other time I was all for woman's empowerment, but I threw that shit out the window as soon I crossed the county line into civilization. My ordeal was over even though I was still a little jumpy. I still had other ways to get my money, so I had to focus on that positive.

"You gotta be fuckin' kidding me." I said aloud.

I didn't need to look at myself in the mirror to see the anger in my eyes. It was all a lie. That place that he'd been taking me to in Atlanta was his playhouse. This was the real thing. Wilton Estates was an upscale, gated community with top-of-the-line, three-story homes that had two-car garages, wrap-around porches, built-in pools, A-line decks, and a lot of secrets. I was mad. Brian wasn't going to get me pregnant, and deny me and my child a good life.

Looking in on his life from the outside, I figured I was entitled to a third, and I wanted everything that was due to me. With all of that being said, I was going to force him to be a man, if it killed me. I stood stone still and played everything over in my head. I knew that everyone was going to have their opinion, on this subject, so I was prepared to wear every label that was going to be pinned on me. But some things weren't easy to get past. I took this on the chin because this wasn't the time to do this. So I got in my car and left. I knew exactly how to strike a nerve because one thing that I knew: there isn't anything more important to a man than his reputation. Brian should have thought about that when I made that first call.

Without looking, I searched for a piece of gum in my bag. The fumes from the shop were making me sick to my stomach, but I was determined to fight through it. *Echelon Hair Studio* sat boldly in the heart of Atlanta. Blocking out the noise and chatter, I looked around at each individual woman trying to figure out who Brian's wife was, by the process of elimination.

"Welcome to Echelon! I'm Sasha. Do you have an appointment with us today?" the cute, petite receptionist asked.

"I'm sorry, I don't. But I have a friend that comes here all the time, and she thinks that I need the magic touch of Traci."

I smiled rubbing my hand through my thick hair. With her long, feathered hair covering her face as she spoke, Sasha looked at me with pity and then began looking through the pink appointment book.

"I'm sorry, but Traci doesn't have an opening until next Tuesday."

"Please, I have my sister's wedding tomorrow . . ." I lied so I could get close to his wife.

I needed to get close to feel out the competition's weaknesses, so I cried into my hands hoping that my efforts wouldn't go overlooked.

"Please, don't cry. Wait here, and I'll see what I can do."

Sasha handed me a tissue. When I felt like she was out of view, I lifted my eyes in a half moon and watched her disappear out of view. Now that I was alone, I really took in all the details of the shop. The cream walls were outlined in a pink-and-grey-leopard print. In the waiting area, a glass table sat on imitation hot-pink, fur rug. While the clients gossiped on the plush-grey, leather sofas, I plotted my next move. Traci had good taste in some areas of her life, but I can't say the same for her poor choice in a husband.

"Um, excuse me . . ."

I turned around, uncertain if I'd gotten in or not.

"Traci says that she can fit you in, but that there will be an additional convenience fee of fifty-dollars."

This is exactly how they got rich. They ripped everyone off, and I wanted my share now that I knew how they really got down. I took out my *Chanel* wallet and handed her the fifty-dollar bill.

"That's fine. I'm just glad that she's going to see me. Besides, my child's father, *Brian*, is funding this."

Sasha's eyes got wide and inquiring. I smiled confirming her thoughts in an indirect way.

"Follow me to the wash station." she said looking back at me.

Everything was going according to plan, and I was getting a step closer to ruining his life. Daydreaming, I held the jeweled-heart-shaped frame in my hand. They looked so happy together. I snickered. How happy could he be if I was having his baby? Traci couldn't satisfy or make him happy, like I could. And as soon as I got the chance I was going to let her know.

Things would definitely be different, if I was in Traci's shoes. If given the chance, I would look damn good in this lifestyle. I touched his face, wishing that everything could have occurred under better circumstances. But it didn't, so I had to make the best of this wild situation.

My attention was diverted from the photo when she cleared her throat. I looked down at the photo again and back to the homely, mature woman standing in front of me. This place was fabulous but this woman was simple, plain, and second-rate. I had to process this picture in my head because I wasn't understanding what Brian ever saw in her.

"I'm sorry. I was just looking at your picture."

Traci let her guard down and put a smile on her clove-colored face. I was trying to be polite but I just couldn't help but to stare. There was nothing attractive about her, like her boyish figure to her slightly sunken-in face that she tried to cover with heavy makeup. There was no competition here, from what I was seeing. So why was I still worried?

"So, what can I do for you today?"

I put the picture down and sat in the chair.

"Something manageable."

"I'll make you happy," she responded parting my hair. "So, who did you say referred you?" she asked.

"I didn't, but its my friend Isis."

"The name doesn't sound familiar. But then again, there are so many people that come in and out of the shop . . . I can't keep up."

"I've been admiring your shops' décor."

"Thank you. I did all of this myself," she said waiving the rattail comb in the air. "In addition to this shop. I have my own design firm, *Syncere Designs*."

"Wow, you have a lot on your plate."

"Yes, I do. On top of all of that I'm the first lady of a mega church."

"Where at?" I caught myself after it slipped out. "I'm sorry. I don't mean to be nosey."

"No, you're perfectly ok. My husband is senior pastor at Zion Worship Center."

"I thought he said it was Deliverance Christian Worship Center." I mumbled, remembering the story he told me.

"Excuse me . . ." she said.

"How is that working out for you?" I replied.

"To be totally honest, it's very stressful. My first job is to support my husband, and that's a very hard thing to do, especially when you have a lot against you."

"Like what?" I asked looking at her through the mirror as she blow dried my hair.

"Church Women! Everybody that sits in those pews on Sunday is not looking for Christ."

"Really . . . is it that bad?"

"Everybody has a different opinion on the subject, but they don't know unless they're in my shoes. Most people just look at the title and the glam behind it, but for me, its hell on earth. While my husband fights with the temptation of the flesh, they bait him with the things of this world."

I shook my head.

"Women can be so disrespectful. They never stop to think, *what if I was in her position?*" she whispered, staring off into a deep gaze. "This one time, at our old church in Dallas, my husband was accused of statutory rape. It was heartbreaking. I didn't know what to do, stick by my husband or get a divorce. Even now, I still don't know if I made the right decision. Anyway, at the time, this little girl was seventeen, and she got herself pregnant. She accused Brian of being the father. He admitted that he took her to a couple of dinners to "mentor" her, but my heart told me that there was a lot more to that chronicle. I saw the receipts to the boutiques and jewelry stores, and the new car he bought for *our daughter.* I know that because I called the dealership. Courtney even knew about the birthmark on his upper thigh. On one end, I believed him because that's what my vows said to do. But the fact is, I married a slimy adulterer and maybe Satan himself. With her help, he allowed everything to teardown our marriage. It was horrible. Everyone knew that she was a fast-tail tramp. But her grandmother just needed to put the blame on someone. If I had to pick the worst chapter in my life, that had to be the worst twenty-nine months of my marriage because Brian left it a long time ago."

"I couldn't envision or want to be in that predicament . . . ever."

My heart broke for her, when I caught this tiny glimpse of what she had to deal with. He was mean and nasty, for no reason.

I don't blame Courtney because I too had suffered the horrible effects of Brian's charm as well. Traci was too soft to go against her husband, but I wasn't. I was going to give him enough hell for the both of us.

"Everyday I questioned if he really "raped" her, and why was she stalking me? She was horrible, calling my job, and sitting outside our home . . . I used to work for the state of Dallas and got fired because of the trouble that she brought to my life. The last time that I saw her, she showed up at my door at five in the morning, screaming, yelling, and cursing. She vandalized my brand-new, 2005 Audi. I had to call the cops."

"Was it his baby?"

"No, and thank God for that blessing. She wouldn't give up though. He told her that he didn't want be with her, and that he wasn't leaving me," she laughed. "They all think that they can replace me, but they can never give him what I give him. Anyway, she took some pills and mixed them with liquor. She died. Even though he wasn't the father his reputation was tarnished forever, and they blamed her death on him. Even today he still has blood on his hands because of his lust addiction."

"Do you think that he loved her?" I asked.

"I don't think that he did. He just wanted what was between her legs. He loves anything that he thinks that he can control and manipulate. He's a man, and he did what he did to get what he wanted. But that relationship wasn't nothing because that young girl had nothing to offer him. I made him who he is today."

"I know exactly what you mean. I'm a couple of weeks along, and the father doesn't want any part of the baby. I know I could have been more careful, but he needs to take care of his responsibilities."

"Sis, I agree."

"I'm glad you feel that way."

That statement went right over her head.

"That's my only sadness." she said in a humble voice.

"What? Not having kids?"

"Yes, it just never seemed like it was God's plan, but now it's too late."

"You never know what fate has in store for you."

"Bless your soul. I'm forty-eight. There is no way a baby is coming from me. And Brian sure better not be coming home with one either. I'm not going through that again."

I got quiet. It didn't matter what she wanted. It was coming in six months, whether she was ready for it or not. I could sympathize with her dilemma, and that's why I couldn't tell her right now. It was a shame that she was going to have to hear this from a total stranger, rather than her own husband.

"But you should make it a priority to visit our church." she offered handing me a card.

"I might have to do that."

I sat in the car, in front of the salon, with the phone pressed up against my ear.

"You don't deserve a wife like Traci because she is too good for you. She told me some interesting things, and your reputation proceeds you." I said looking into the mirror as I smoothed a stray piece of hair back into place.

"You bitch! Stay away from my wife!"

"That's a damn joke because she seems to like me and our unborn child. She has the desire to help the needy and that's me since you abandoned me in my fragile state. And since my baby's father is a bum, she's going to help me in anyway she can. I might ask her to be the Godmom, so Brian listen to this. I'm not staying away because of the fact that I'm carrying your baby. Now, get used to the fact that I'm going to be around for a long time. Bye." I antagonized before hanging up the phone.

As soon as I entered the building the security guard had a crowd around him. I stood at the elevator looking over some of Brian's text messages. He always tried to make me out to be crazy. But the messages clearly let me know that our entire relationship wasn't a figment of my wild imagination.

"*Yeah, the police is at the dental office on the sixteenth floor. They waiting for the receptionist to come in. They have her on camera stealing pain meds . . .*" the gossiping guard said.

My heart was laying on the freshly waxed floor when I slid out of the door just as quietly as I came in. It was crazy how I had a partner in all of this but was going to have to take the fall alone if

I went upstairs. When I woke up this morning I never knew that my three years at this job was going to end today. Oh well, it was better than having to go back to jail, especially when I was facing a bid.

13

I didn't think this out at all. Once minute I was at home catching up on some much needed housework and now I'm here. I stood on the porch and said nothing. Jeremy was looking good to me, now that I was running through my savings and was pregnant by another man. I was going to win him back and let him think that this baby I'm carrying is his. It's a little believable because if I looked closely, him and Brian resembled each other.

"Mia, what are your doing here?" Jeremy asked.

I've been at his mother's house plenty of times before, but the guilt behind what I did to him kept me from going inside. Besides, I knew his mother knew everything that happened between us and if she caught me in her house she would have skinned me alive for breaking her baby boy's heart.

"I needed to see you."

I knew how he felt about me, but his don't-give-a-damn vibe that he was giving off told me that he had enough of my shit.

"You seeing me, now what?"

"I deserve this and more. I wasn't right how I treated you. Let me take you to get something to eat so that we can talk some more."

"I guess I'll be funding that to . . . ." he said sarcastically. "You know what, I can't even look at you right now."

"I'm sorry. Please give me a chance to make things right, because I know that you want that to." I begged.

During the drive to Sylvie's, I had a chance to think about my rekindling a faithful relationship with Jeremy. Although he was broke as hell, and couldn't offer me the title of *First Lady*, he was convenient, reliable and durable, sort of like a trash bag. I didn't have to gamble on this sure-shot.

"I thought I made you happy?" he asked not touching his plate of beef short-ribs, spinach and macaroni-and-cheese."

I swallowed the food in my mouth before I spoke.

"You did, in the beginning. But when you started ignoring me and putting other people and things before me, that pushed me away . . ."

"I'm sorry, I really didn't know I hurt you. How come you just didn't come and talk to me instead of leaving me, and stealing from me?"

"Because I thought that you would have eventually come to your senses and made everything right. I just couldn't believe that we been together that long and things turned out like this."

"You didn't help matters by cheating on me."

"I didn't . . ."

Just as soon as I was about to tell my version, I saw Solae walking towards the table with a grin on her face.

"What is the likelihood of me running into you here? You must have been reading my mind that I needed to talk to you."

"About what?" I asked.

Before she focused on me she turned to Jeremy.

"Hey boo!"

She hugged him.

"Its been a long time. When did y'all get back together?" she asked minding my business.

"What do you mean by that?" he asked.

"Nothing," I intervened. "What is it that you wanted to see me about?"

"Do you want me to do this here?"

"I don't have nothing to hide."

"Something hit me after I left your house and our phone conversation the other day. What really went down between you and Brian on Valentine's Day?"

"Why are you drudging up old shit! That happened over four months ago." I said.

"But the information you're withholding from me is new. And you need to be a woman about yours and tell me what the real truth is!"

"I'm tired of you coming at me with the same voided subject," I said standing from my seat. "I know the real truth, but if you don't believe me then, that's on you!"

"Ladies, this ain't the time or place for this. Solae, if Mia says that nothing happened between her and Brian, then nothing happened." Jeremy said coming to my defense.

"Time will tell all." she said before she turned and walked away.

Recounting everything that has happened, I still couldn't believe that Solae put this Brian subject on front street so that Jeremy could have a chance to question my loyalty. But being the conniving bitch that she is, she did just that. Now I needed to find a way to minimize my involvement in this situation. I'm just glad that she didn't have a chance to mention the fact that I was pregnant.

"Do you want this to work?" he asked ignoring Solae's accusations.

"Um hum."

"Then I need for you to lay everything out on the table, before we can move on."

"The only thing that you need to know is that I love you."

It was funny to me that he wanted to talk now, after I tried so hard to compromise with him before. I knew that the only reason that he was at my door was because I had direct contact with his wife. Little did he know that visiting me wasn't going to stop me from getting what I wanted and needed for my child. My curiosity wouldn't let me ignore him, so I put the chain on the door and opened it.

"Yes." I said looking through the door.

"Can I come in?"

"Not really 'cause I'm not looking to entertain your bullshit tonight." I said.

"There are a lot of things that we need to discuss."

"You're so full of shit that it ain't funny. Just last week I was bitches and hoes, and now we need to talk."

I laughed.

"I know why you're here, so to save you a headache, this is what I'm going to do. I'm gonna' raise this baby alone. See you in court."

I pushed the door with my foot when he stuck his arm inside. I sucked my teeth and rolled my eyes.

"Please let me in. I did a lot of thinking, and I left her to be with you."

This was the first time that I heard him say this. I took the chain off and naively let him in. Looking at Brian was making me mad all over again. How can I deny what he said to me? In my heart, I wanted to believe that he was being sincere, but I knew that he was only here because I threatened to expose his "sanctified" ass. Now he needed to keep me close to make certain that I was going to keep his dirty secret. Now that I know everything, my plan was to play his game, to an extent. If I kept him fearful, then I'd get everything that I wanted.

"So, what's really so damn important that you had to come here at 2:36 in the morning?" I asked looking at the clock on the mantel.

"Before you continue, don't lie."

"I'm being completely honest. My things are in the car . . . . I left my wife." he said.

I humored him, went to my window, and opened the curtains. As surely as he was standing there, the midnight-blue Acura was filled with three large suitcases. I turned back around and faced him.

"You thought that I was lying?"

"Hell yeah!" I spoke honestly. That's all you'd been doing ever since I met you."

"Well, I'm not. Things haven't been right between us for a very long time. It's not a good look for the leader of a mega church to leave his wife."

"Well, things haven't changed in that area, so why are you here?"

"Because some things are more important. I prayed long and hard about this." he said rubbing my small bump.

"Why don't I believe you?"

"Because I haven't been truthful about everything. I apologize for everything that I said and did to you."

I was over his apologies because he was spending them like a penny with a hole in it.

"What about the baby?" I asked because he forgot to mention that important piece of information.

"Are you hungry?"

"Don't skip the subject."

"Babe, its not that serious. Relax. We are going to pray for your patience."

"If that's the case, I need to go to church . . . . With you."

He scratched his head, looking around trying to avoid eye contact.

"See. You are so full of shit. I see what this is hitting for . . ." I said angry that I fell for nothing.

"No, I'm not. It's just that I can't disgrace my church or hurt my wife anymore than I already have by parading you around town, especially with a baby that she wanted."

"With that being said, I'm going to ask you again. What in the hell are you doing here?"

"Because this is where I want to be. Let me go get my things."

I sat on the sofa and shook my head. I had a lot of decisions to make. I was in my junior year at *CAU*, pregnant with the baby of a married preacher who had left his wife to play house with me. But that was all minor compared to what I had to do now. I had to tell my strict, traditional father what I'd gotten myself into. Of course I was going to leave out most of the heartbreaking details which would make him disown me.

My hands trembled as I texted the first words. If I told him face-to-face, then he would kill me. I could picture the hurt on his distressing face. He hoped that I would become a lawyer, but now that dream was shot. Brian walked back in the door at the same moment I sent my confession.

"What's wrong babe?"

"Nothing. I'm just tired."

That was an understatement.

"I'm just gonna' come right out and say this."

I looked up at him. Here it was, the reason why he really came here.

"I really think that you need to get an abortion." he blurted out.

He reached into his pocket and held out a piece of paper. I didn't take it, so he sat it on my lap.

"I set up an appointment for you. Of course, I'll be with you when you get the procedure done. Don't worry about anything, because I'm paying for everything. I decided that this is best for the both of us. I love you, and I don't want you to think that the only reason why I'm here is out of obligation. So, once you get it done, we can do things the right way, the second time around."

Before I got a chance to respond, there was a knock at the door. Brian looked from me back to the door. I hunched my shoulders because I wanted him to ignore the door, just this one time.

"If you think that you are gonna' have strange men coming in here, doing God knows what, then you have another thing coming!" he said through gritted teeth.

"You don't have to get it. That's my past." I said sadly.

I couldn't believe what had came out of my mouth. How quickly I was forgetting what I promised Jeremy just because some *good catch* slithered his back way into my life with nicely wrapped bullshit. I knew that Jeremy loved me unconditionally but that wasn't enough. Brian ignored every word that I said. He stood at the door acting as the man of my house and my life. I couldn't do this. I found my body pressed up against the lilac kitchen wall listening.

"What is it that you need this time of morning?" Brian asked.

"Dude, I don't know who you are, but this is my girlfriend's home."

"What is that suppose to mean to me? I'm here now, and that's my baby she's carrying. So hell no I don't want no strange men in here."

"Baby! Mia! What the fuck is he saying? What is going on?" Jeremy yelled.

This mild-mannered man went from zero to sixty in seconds. I couldn't face this now that everything was out in the open. I thought that if I didn't see it then it would be easier to deal with, but the effects of hearing it hurt just the same.

"What the fuck are you talking about?! A baby! Man get the fuck out of here!" he yelled. "Yo, Mia! Come out here and face me like a woman! I know you hiding!"

I wasn't going to face him. If I had my way not now, not ever. I peaked my head around the corner and watched the men in my life throwing body blows to each other. This went from bad to worst. The lamp crashed to the floor. Brian gripped Jeremy around his neck and strong-armed him out of my life. My body was shaking so bad that my teeth chattered. I fell to the floor crying uncontrollably. He was gone. Jeremy's pounding intensified when Brian made his point clearly. Now that I was getting exactly what I wanted, why does it feel wrong?

"You are going to do exactly what I say from this point on." Brian said looking down at me.

14

An abortion? It wasn't enough for Brian to suggest one, but he also made the appointment, expecting me to agree to it. It's clear that he thought that I would just agree to his every wish. Brian should have known that this was also a sin. But, I shouldn't have expected any morals from a man that constantly cheats on his wife. I had already made up my mind when I told my father about the new addition to our family, my decision is final. All that I've been through with Brian is making me question why I want to have his baby in the first place.

"This is nothing but drama." I whispered.

"Mia, what is wrong with you?" My cousin asked.

It would be easier for me to tell her what was right with me because that list was very short. I turned and faced Kim. I decided to let her know what had been going on now that I was having a mental breakdown in our criminology class.

"Please, don't cry. I hate to see you like this." she whispered, wiping my tears away with her hand before anyone could notice.

"I'm pregnant."

She didn't say anything as her disappointed, grey eyes looked down at me with pity.

"What . . . when . . . ."

"It's not by who you think it is."

Kim held up her hand. This was the second person in my life that I didn't want to disappoint. Kim Jordan is my first cousin on my mother's side. She grew up in Northeast Philly. She spent summers with me in Sugar Hill which made being the only child tolerable. I turned away from her baby face because I knew that my next words would confirm to Kim the type of person I really was.

"On Valentine's Day, Solae . . ."

"Say no more."

I knew that Kim didn't want to hear anything I had to say, especially pertaining to Solae. She had drilled into my head that dealing with my best friend was going to get me a one way ticket to hell with a few detours to nowhere.

"Please, I been holding this in for a while. Solae needed to use my place, so I had to entertain Brian until she got there. That night we ended up having sex before she got there. And it has been going on since February."

I lifted up my pink *Old Navy* sweatshirt just enough for her to see my bump. Kim reached out and then took it back quickly. I took her hand and placed it on my stomach, reassuring her that this was as real as it got.

"What . . ." she said sympathetically.

"Wait, there's more."

Her eyes deepened as she continued to rub on my stomach.

"He's married."

"Mia . . ."

"And he's a pastor of a mega church . . . and it's triplets."

"Oh God!"

"And I met his wife."

"What?" her voice echoed.

"She don't know about this or me, but I just had to see her."

"What is wrong with you? This is so beneath you." she judged.

"He moved in with me a few nights ago because he left her to build with me."

"Don't y'all know that y'all playing a dangerous game? And what type of Pastor is he to do something so nasty? I feel sorry for his poor wife." she said shaking her head.

"What about me?" I asked needing sympathy.

"You know better," she sighed. "But I don't love you any less," she said putting her arm around me. "I'm gonna' be here and support you regardless. What did Uncle William say?"

"I don't know. I texted him and told him. He called like thirty times and left a few dozen messages. I didn't bother to listen to any of them. I just have that gut feeling that I know what he is gonna' say, because I know him. But that's the least of my worries. Brian told me to get an abortion."

"Well?" she asked.

"I don't know. It's three blessings. Things like this don't happen for no reason."

"Three," she whispered. "Does he know about it?"

"No."

"Well, you know that this is a part of his game."

"Are you asking me or telling me?"

"I'm telling you. Brian don't love you or want to be with you. And he sure as hell didn't leave his wife for you. Trust and believe it. This is the oldest trick in the book. I love you, but why would he mess up his happy home for a child? Especially if his wife is totally oblivious about you?"

I didn't have a response for that because the truth hurt. I guess I believed the fantasy so much that I couldn't see past what Brain told me.

"He told you to get rid of the baby so that y'all can have a chance . . . right?"

It was as if she had sat in on our conversation that day. I was speechless for a moment. I shook my head verifying what she suspected.

"That's what he said, he thinks it's one baby . . ." I managed to get out.

"I know, and that is a damn lie. He just don't want the scandal or the child support order, especially for one, let alone three. He was with y'all arrangement as long as he could hit and run without the responsibility. Now with babies involved, he's not standing for that. Take it from me. When they say that they gonna' leave their wife, they never do."

Kim stared off into space like she was speaking from an experienced past.

"You . . ."

"Yes, except for the fact that mine was my neighbor."

My perfect cousin had a dark past. Her confession challenged what I thought I knew. Kim and I were so close. Her choosing to have left me out of that part of her life stunned me. From the outside looking in, she was perfect. She had the perfect grades, popularity, two parents, beauty, as well as skeletons in her walk-in closet. Kim was no better than me, so I didn't have to pretend anymore.

The conversation that I had with Kim stayed with me. My eyes wouldn't leave Brian's bag sitting in the corner of my bedroom. He didn't waste anytime making himself at home. The temptation to go through his things was mentally exhausting. What if I found something that would ruin what we were *trying to do*? I just had to take the chance and deal with the outcome later.

I slid off the paisley charcoal comforter onto the floor. I pulled the smallest bag towards me. I had the opportunity to leave the issue alone and just trust the man who proved to me more than once that he couldn't be trusted. The soft suede bag rested on my lap, and I opened it. The church's information didn't catch my attention as much as the white, letter-sized envelope. My paranoia increased along with the beating of my aching heart.

I wasn't the only one, and I held the burning truth in my hand. Along with a few ultrasound pictures, were two baby registries for Desiree Abrams. There was no doubt that Brian didn't think that this child wasn't his. I pitied my unborn babies. They weren't even here yet, and they were being rejected by Brian. What made her child more important than mine? I didn't have the answer to it, but I was going to find out.

"How long have you been seeing Brian?" I asked before losing my nerve.

I never spoke with this person before, so I didn't know what I was up against. All I knew was that I had something to get off of my chest.

"Who is this?"

"I'm Brian's pregnant girlfriend."

"Aw shit!" the raspy voice yelled into my ear.

"May I ask how old are you?" I asked as if it really mattered.

"No, you can't! You have the nerve to call my phone and stir up this pot full of trouble. And you ask me how old I am? Little girl, I'm old enough to know that you shouldn't be ringing my number. You should be ringing your boyfriend's neck," she said. "If he's your man." she insinuated.

"You're right. I'm sorry for bothering you. I was just looking through his things and . . ."

"Baby girl, when you go searching, you might just find everything that you're looking for. You didn't need to search for what you already knew in your heart."

The wisdom caused me more misery. This hurt more than I expected it to, and I prepared myself beforehand.

"Are you there?" she asked.

I swallowed the hard lump of certainty, and in a low whisper I responded.

"Yes."

"In my sixty years . . ."

My chest deflated because there was no way in hell that she was pregnant, old as she was.

"I been in enough shit with all types of gigolos and no good niggas to know that if you were in my shoes, it would have eaten you alive. Look at you now, crying over a man that only cares about one thing . . . himself. It reminds me of this one named Joe. I was so in love with his fine ass. I loved him to death. There wasn't anything that I wouldn't do for him even sell my body, when he suggested it. So, I know how you feel. Whoever said that love doesn't hurt, sure as hell haven't loved before." she spoke in a faint voice.

"I'm sorry." was the only thing that came out of my mouth.

"Babe, don't feel sorry for me. Feel sorry for your boyfriend cause when I get 'hold of him, I'm gonna' put another hole in his black ass."

"Wait, I thought."

"No you assumed, mistake number one. Brian has been with my granddaughter Neiva for four years, and she's pregnant with his child. And he wanted this."

"How do you know he wanted it? There are two sides to every story." I said trying to give him the benefit of the doubt.

"Cause, he come here cryin' on my shoulders about it. I know that sneaky shit he did to make this happen. He poked holes in the condoms, hid her pills . . . he defiantly wanted this. When you confront him, which I know you are, don't let him sell you another dream. You deserve better."

This pregnancy was sucking the life out of me, or was it what the pregnancy represented that had me depressed? Neiva's grandmother's words joined Kim's words. After half an hour in a fog, I finally made my way down the hall hoping that a shower would clear my mind.

Certain things needed to be established from the beginning. I dropped the ball on that concept. Brian thought that he was going to do whatever he damned well pleased because I let him do that ever since we met. Now, here I was at six in the morning waiting for him to come home. So that he wouldn't be able to sneak in and pretend that he'd been on the couch the entire night, I put the arm chair in front of the door, crossed my legs and waited for my boyfriend to make an appearance.

I fought through my fatigue because I needed to get my built-up anger out in the open. I couldn't sleep even if I wanted to, so I went into the bedroom to watch TV. I just couldn't understand what Brain was gaining from stringing me along.

The nightmare of Traci hunting me down for sleeping with her husband made me break out into a cold sweat. When she cornered me in the alley behind the church, she put the .22 up to my chest which scared the hell out of me because I knew that my end was near. Sweat was pouring from my face as I pleaded for my life when Brian walked up behind us. I begged again, but this time, it was for his help. He didn't say a single word when he patted Traci on the back. She turned back towards me with hate on her face and pulled the trigger.

I put my hand over the area where the hole should have been. I wiped my forehead. It was 5:43 p.m. and no message or call from Brian that would put my mind at ease. I calmed myself enough to make my way to the kitchen for some lemonade. I stood at the door frozen in the moment.

His pants were around his ankles while a woman, disrespectfully laid across my kitchen table moaning in enjoyment. His actions consumed me with every emotion in the book. While his body smacked against hers sounding like someone popping bubble gum, I couldn't breath. The mixture of lust and fresh peaches nauseated me. Her black skirt was up around her waist while he continued knocking her off, in my house . . . in my kitchen, where I ate. I couldn't, wait let me rephrase that, I didn't want to believe that he was that damn disrespectful, bold . . . just nasty. I wiped my eyes so hard that they burned.

"What the fuck!" I yelled snapping out of my state of shock.

She opened her eyes to find out that they weren't alone.

"Wait Mia, stop! I can explain everything!"

She scrambled to get herself out of the position that she was in. My sweaty hand was full of blond hair. I pulled her off my fouled table which now had to be burnt. When I pulled her ass onto my floor I saw her red lace thongs. Bitches were so foul and grimy, and I was going to put my foot so far up her ass that when she thought about crossing me again she would think twice.

I didn't care that I was pregnant because the rage consumed me, taking on a life of its own. Brian tried to separate us. Every time I banged her head against the floor, her screams increased. I blacked out.

"Get off of me!" I yelled kicking to get free.

Brian held me around my waist while I wiggled to get free. The intruder got off my floor and smacked me right in my face while he still held me tight. This time when I kicked it landed between his legs. Brian dropped me on the floor where I was eye to eye with her panties. What came next was going to change things forever. Brian kicked me in the stomach.

15

My vision was blurry, and my head was pounding. This place wasn't familiar to me. I was disoriented. Trying to figure out where I was added to the anxiety. All I could remember was my last conversation. I rubbed my teary eyes, setting off rapid bells. Brian and Kim were on either side of my bed.

"Where am I?"

"Boo, you're in the hospital. Do you remember what happened?" Kim asked moving my hair out of my face.

"I came home and found her on the kitchen floor." he answered.

"I wasn't talking to you." she said.

"I think you better leave!" Brian yelled at my cousin causing me to shutter.

"I think you better leave with your lying ass! If she "fell" then how did she get that black eye?" Kim questioned.

Her comment caused me to think. Black eye . . . I thought patting my eyes. Things were vague in the beginning but hearing him talk brought everything back. Because I remembered, I turned my heavy head, staring at him with emotional pain.

"Oh, you believe her over me?" he asked responding to my body language.

"Hell yeah she believes me, because that's some bullshit you standing over there talking!"

"You stupid child!" he belittled.

I sat up ready to start what I finished. He never seemed to amaze me. But one thing was for sure: family stick together and he had the wrong woman if he thought that he was going to disrespect Kim.

"Don't talk to her like that you nasty bastard! If you weren't fuckin' that bitch in my kitchen, then I wouldn't even be here!" I yelled causing me to get lightheaded.

"I knew it was a mistake to get a ghetto piece of trash like you pregnant. You would believe anything . . . huh . . . I should have known because you actually believed that I would leave a successful, well-off, educated woman for a nobody like you." he shot coldly.

Brian shook his head looking at me like I was sewage.

"I think you need to get the hell outta' here before I really light up your world . . . if you get my drift."

This was the first time that I saw my dad in two months. Although I wished that Brian and his chick didn't attack me, these circumstances made facing my father easier.

"Daddy."

He walked over to the bed, ignoring me completely. It was apparent that he had to handle a major problem, before he dealt with me.

"Lay back Mia. Don't protect the man that put you in here and could have caused you to lose your babies." Kim announced.

"Babies!" Brian and my dad yelled at the same time.

"Yeah, triplets." she answered.

My dad looked flustered while Brian's face looked angry.

I wasn't listening to anything that she had to say. I wasn't protecting him, but I didn't want Brian to have any excuse to escape his responsibilities.

"You need to stay out of this 'cause you don't even know me!" Brian yelled lashing out from the news.

"Dude, I don't have to know you, but that's my daughter and unborn grandchildren there," my dad said pointing at me without even looking into my direction. "So if someone is causing them issues then it's my problem."

Despite my father's overbearing nature, the last thing that I wanted to do was hurt him or put him in any danger. The situation was escalating, and neither of them were willing to back down. My father, at fifty-three-years-old, was standing fearless against my thirty-four-year-old mistake. He was staring at Brian directly in the eyes.

"Old man, don't let me lay my religion down! I swear, if you threaten me again then I will have you locked up only after I beat you the fuck up!"

"If you touch my daughter again, I will kill you. Make no mistake about it." my father said through gritted teeth.

"Well, your daughter needs to find the father of those babies cause they're not mine. Triplets don't even run in my family. And if she slept with me the first time that we met, then the likelihood is that this is her normal routine. You should have taught her to keep her damn legs closed."

"I swear if you say another word against my daughter, then so help me God!"

"Don't worry. That nasty bitch ain't worth my words."

Brian pushed past my father, never looking in my direction. Knowing him for only an hour, I made the choice to have sex with him proceeding his numerous blows, but this was different because now my father had to bear the humiliation of my poor judgment.

"I'm not thrilled about you having a kids at such a young age, but we can't take that back. I'm going to help you because you are going to finish college and my grandkids deserves a good life. But, if I find out that you taken' back up with that son-of-a-bitch, you will be cut off, and I will disown you." My father said looking down at me harshly.

I knew that he meant what he said.

After spending a week in the hospital and knowing that my babies were okay, I was glad to finally be home. Although I'm suppose to be on bed rest, I had to get rid of my dad and reject his constant offers for me to go back to his house. But I was missing Brian, and I wanted to see if we could work things out, because what went down was obviously a misunderstanding. That's why I needed to be home, alone.

I headed to the bedroom after I saw confirmation that I might not be getting what I wanted anytime soon. Brian had moved all his stuff out of my home. He took my flat screen, *Gucci* luggage, three-hundred dollars, all of my mother's jewelry, a roll of toilet paper, and three T-bone steaks. I held my breath when I saw that all he'd left in my closet was a cat costume from last Halloween. He just wouldn't let up on me.

Zora's wasn't a place that I'd expect an uppity man like Brian to be caught dead in, let alone a place where he'd take his wife for her birthday. Despite seeing how many people were in here, I had to do this. If they knew everything, I'm sure they would agree with my method. My eyes landed on every face in the restaurant. My mouth got dry when I focused on Brian and his wife, sitting at a cozy table near the back of the restaurant. Before I knew it, my legs were moving, and I was walking towards them.

My mind was blank while my emotions ran high. Brian held her hand, looking deep into her bugged eyes. He thought that his troubles had passed, but little did he know they were just beginning. I stood directly in front of them, shaking my head. The thought of him using my money to fund their outing irritated me. I picked up the roses from the table, smelled them, shedding some of the pretty petals, and dropped them back onto the table.

"Please don't get up on my account." I said pulling up a chair joining the father of my children and his wife.

I sat the envelope on the table next to Traci, and she stared at it. She looked at her husband and then back to me. I was a little sorry that I was doing this, especially on her birthday, but I cared about my future more than her feelings. Brian looked fearful for the first time since I met him, and that didn't phase me. He was a hot mess, covered in an expensive suit. Brian wasn't concerned with anything but protecting his secret. What I laid on the table was going to let every truth be told. That's why I brought proof.

"Mia . . ." she mumbled. "Brian, what is this?" Traci asked squinting at me.

"I think that we need to go. I'll explain it in the car."

Traci pulled away from him when he tried to control her and the situation. I took his plate of string beans, potato salad, and turkey wings and started eating. He got up but she remained mentally paralyzed. I wiped my mouth before speaking.

"Everything that you need to know is right here . . . it's self-explanatory."

I tapped the envelope with the handle of the fork. If looks could actually kill, I would have been murdered right where I sat. I could feel the fire rising from the devil as he stood motionless. Holding her chest, Traci gasped, and tears wouldn't stop rolling down her face.

"You stupid bitch!" he yelled drawing attention to the table.

"Really? You got me pregnant and came to my house telling lies, but I'm the stupid bitch! And this sure as hell don't look like you left her to me!"

"I hate you!" he yelled.

"Yeah, I know. The feeling is mutual. Maybe she have enough sense to leave your cheating ass now!"

Everything, on the table, crashed to the floor. Traci looked as if she'd lost her mind. The fork stayed in my hand as I scrambled to move out of her way.

"You dirty nigga you! Triplets!"

"Triplets!" he repeated lethargically.

"You ain't nothing but a low-life, nasty, son-of-a-bitch! I made you who you are! When I met you, you was nothing but a little-ass boy, flipping burgers, sleeping on yo' mama's couch! You ain't know a damn thing 'bout the good life! And you goin' to do this to me again! I promised you after that shit in Dallas that if you ever did this again, then I was gonna kill you dead nigga!" she spewed.

Everything that Traci had built up in her, from years of Brian's philandering, exploded like rapid gunfire. Things went from bad to worse when she tried to stab him with a steak knife. This wasn't my fight, so I stepped back just in case she turned her anger towards me.

16

Hormones had nothing to do with the fact that I didn't sleep all night and had been crying non-stop. Jeremy in his bitter spitefulness had put me out of my apartment. The Sheriffs were so heartless and inconsiderate to the fact that I was pregnant. I was only allowed to grab whatever I could and nothing more. Jeremy's face was blank. He refused to look at me as he sat in his two-year-old Range Rover. He watched silently while they took my world from under me. I never thought that I could despise a person as much as I hated Jeremy now. I just never thought that if I played with fire, then I'd eventually get burnt. Oh well, I can't take back the past.

Torn down by Jeremy and Brian for two very different reasons, I drove around Sugar Hill for hours, hungry and tired. I felt like the prodigal daughter as I sat in front of my childhood home on Chambery Drive. I wasn't in the position to choose between my child's father and my father. I wanted them both. Burdened, I tried erasing the signs of stress from my face although it remained internally. Every man that I loved showed me that the only thing that they wanted was to control me. I just didn't want that stronghold over me any more. Left without a place to go, I had to reconsider my rash decision to be independent because the thought of being homeless scared the hell out of me. This arrangement was going to have to do for now.

Staying in my childhood room with the pink-flowered walls and Barbie dolls, perched on their shelves, didn't bring back many happy moments. All it represented was loneliness. I hugged my knees, crying into them because it had to be better than this. To me, there wasn't anything worse than being alone. This time, I couldn't go into my dad's room and curl up beside him because he was away on business. After debating with myself, I knew that I couldn't make it through the night without him, so I dialed his number.

"Can you stay the night with me? I need you."

I held my breath and waited for him to speak.

"After you ruined my life, you need me?" Brain laughed.

"I needed a way to get your attention to let you know that I was serious about us."

That was partly true. I had to say whatever it took to get what I needed.

"Where are you?"

I smiled at the unexpected response.

"I'm at my father's house."

"Didn't he threaten that if you stayed with me, he'd disown you?"

"Yes, but . . ." I meekly responded regretting I told him what was said.

"He's out of town, so you don't have nothing to worry about."

"Baby, I'm not worried. I love it when people challenge me and forbid me to do something. Text me the address and give me an hour."

The lavender-lace boy shorts didn't catch his attention, and neither did the fact that I came to the door completely naked. Brian sat on the single sofa texting and not paying any attention to me. I guess he felt like he did his charity work just by coming here, and that everything else was extra. I knelt at his feet removing the phone from his hand. I knew that I needed companionship, but I never thought that I would be this excited to see the man who was having sex with another woman in my own apartment and tried to kill our children. My time was always limited with him, so I had to make the best of it.

"Go somewhere." he said snatching the phone from me.

"All I wanted to do was spend some time with you. You must have felt the same because you're here."

"Just because I came don't mean shit!" he snapped. "Stop thinking that it's more between us than it is. Damn!"

"Why are you so mean to me all the time? Why don't you want me? I don't deserve this, especially now that I'm having your babies."

I knew that his attitude had nothing to do with me, but I took it to heart.

"Yeah about that. Why are you trying to hold onto something that will never be. I got with you for one reason and that was to get the pussy. Now that I got it, and you're pregnant, I don't want you or those bastards you're carrying or your used coochie. Fuck y'all!" Brian hissed.

My heart stopped beating. Brian said some mean shit to me before, but it wasn't anything compared to what had just come out of his mouth. The intensity from his body forced me away as I landed on the floor at his feet like a pile of rubbish.

"See now, you gave me a headache, go get me something."

Without responding, I got up and went up the stairs. I sat on the side of the bathtub and contemplated calling Kim, although I knew how she felt about Brian. I needed to talk to someone, but it couldn't be her. I couldn't let her know that I was weak enough to fall for an abusive, no good, and disrespectful man. Instead, I snapped the lid to the Excedrin closed and went downstairs.

I noticed that Brian wasn't where I left him.

"Shit!" his voice echoed from the kitchen.

His shadow moved across the wall when he peeked out the door. I ducked in the darkness so that he wouldn't see me. I tipped around the creeks in the steps that I'd familiarized myself with when I was a teen. Brian ignored the orange juice that he spilled on the counter and focused on refilling the cup with more juice. I held my mouth when I saw him take a small vial out of his pocket and pour it into one of the glasses.

"He's trynna' kill me." I mouthed.

I headed back to the steps walking down with heavy thuds. At the same time, he came out of the kitchen with the two cups.

"Here's your Excedrin." I said handing him the two pills, wishing it was rat poison.

"I got you some juice."

I took the cup and examined it. His eyes never left me. Brian took our relationship to an all time breaking point. What hurt me the most was knowing that someone out there hated me enough to try to kill me. The fear alone caused the wet glass to slip out of my hand, crashing to the floor.

Brian never said a word for the rest of the night, and neither did I. If he was going to pretend like he didn't try to kill my kids last night, then I wasn't going to let him know that I knew either. Because the third time might be a charm.

My eyes were so heavy that it felt like bricks were tied to them. Sleeping wasn't an option around him, but his snoring was taking me there. I kept watching him as he slept, not letting my guard down for one second. Besides, this time allowed me time to think of ways to end his life because it was either him or me.

Brian was gone when I opened my eyes. I jumped out of bed and ran down the hallway to see if he was in the bathroom. He wasn't.

"Daddy, you scared me. When did you get home?" I asked.

"In enough time to see that sleazy nigga leaving my house. What have I told you about him? You deserve better than that trash!" he yelled causing my ears to ring.

"Please daddy, I don't need any of your lectures. I already been through enough."

"I stand by what I say. I think you need to find somewhere else to stay."

"Are you serious?"

My father opened the door, allowing me to see my bags on the front porch.

"As long as you continue to stay with him, your life is going to be hell on earth." he predicted.

"Well, it can't be worst than you kicking me out in the street five-months pregnant. So, I'll take my chances."

17

If anyone thinks that I am going to take anymore of their bullshit, from this day forward, then they need to know that payback is gonna' be bad for them. The old me is back and somewhat lucid. Pregnant or not, I'm starting at the top of my list.

"Mia, Solae isn't here." Daniel said as I invited myself into their five-bedroom custom built home in Savannah.

"I assumed so, but I'm not here to see her anyway."

I shut the door behind me. Immediately I noticed the change in the room. Solae had been at it again spending money that she never earned. Everything in the extra-large living room was platinum leather and trimmed with sterling silver. Hints of turquoise accents popped throughout the room. I watched Solae gold-dig her way to the top. I had learned nothing because if I had, I wouldn't be homeless.

"It's about your wife."

Daniel's slender body lost its balance and landed in a cream wing chair.

"Oh no. It's nothing like that." I informed him quickly.

I watched his chest move slowly like a gentle breeze now that he knew that nothing had happened to his trophy wife. Maybe after he heard what I had to say, he might second guess his original feelings.

"Then what is it?"

"Your wife has been cheating on you. It has been a moral struggle for me because she is my best friend, and my loyalty is to her. But she ain't right."

I never seen a man crumble in front of me, and it wasn't a pretty sight. His beige face turned red like a chili pepper. Daniel's aqua-green eyes watered as he started bawling uncontrollably as if his life was ending. I rubbed his back.

"I knew she was, but I couldn't prove it. Now you confirmed things for me." he said dabbing his red eyes with his shirttail.

"Yeah its true, but did you know that she was pregnant?"

His eyes got wide.

"But she got an abortion. She told me that the twin investments were good enough for her." I spoke truthfully.

"Who is he?" he said in an unrecognizable voice. "Who's been fucking my wife?"

Anger flowed out of his mouth like rusted daggers.

"All I know is that his name is Brian and . . ."

"Where is this Brian? When I catch up to him, I'm going to kill him! That bastard is going to regret the day that he stuck his dick in my wife."

Maybe there are two sides to a person because Daniel got straight hood on me in seconds. It was kind of entertaining and corny at the same time.

"Listen, don't worry about him or her. The two of them are made for each other."

"I'm not trynna' hear that shit sis! What would you do if you found out that your man was cheating?" he asked.

That was the story of my life, so I ignored his question.

"Exactly, I can't believe that this is happening. We have a family together!"

He shook his head that sported his military cut.

Daniel pounded on the arm of the chair. Before he knew what had hit him, I was straddling him and stuck my tongue in his mouth. White men did nothing for me, and I definitely knew that he did nothing for Solae either. But she was only attracted to the bulge in his pocket instead of his pants. And I was only interested in ruining Solae's perfect life.

"Girl have you lost your damn mind! I don't want you. I want my wife!" he yelled as if my gestured repulsed him.

"Why? The only reason why she's with you is for your money. And she cheats on you every chance she gets. Don't you want to get even? The only way to do that is sleep with me."

"No, I don't. I want my wife. I'll take my chances with her." he sniffed.

"Then you're stupid ass will get exactly what you deserve."

Rejection was a bitch no matter what form it came in, period. Being rejected by a skinny, no swag, insignificant, white boy, I knew that I was losing the battle to conquer and destroy.

He shook his head.

"I'm sorry. I shouldn't have said that. But I need a favor. The drive is too long for me to take tonight. Can I stay here?" I asked.

He was skeptical, especially after what I had done. Daniel didn't have to worry about me trying that a second time. I planted the seed, and it was going to sprout to my specifications. All I had to do was watch it grow.

"Take the guestroom. But you have to leave first thing in the morning."

"I promise."

"I don't give a damn who she is!" Solae yelled outside of the bedroom door, before she rushed in on me.

"Bitch get the fuck up!"

I sat up in the bed rubbing my stomach. I stared at her not saying a word. I knew that Solae was aware of what I had done, but I didn't care.

"You know damn good and well that I don't have no bitch laying up in my house!" she continued.

"I didn't have no where else to go."

"That's not my fuckin' problem!"

My best friend let her uncensored wrath out on me, and the true reason behind it was unspoken. But between the two of us, we knew what was going on as her husband stood in front of us, looking unsure of what was actually going on. Solae grabbed hold of my overnight bag, opened the window, and threw it onto the dew covered lawn.

"Solae what has gotten into you!" Daniel yelled, grabbing hold of her arm.

She snatched away and started pushing me.

"Its not what you think!" he yelled at her. "It was just a little misunderstanding."

"Please, don't do this to me." I whispered.

She looked into my eyes, unfazed by what was being said.

"You dirty bitch. I told you that if I found out that you fucked with mine, then I was going to hurt you."

"It happened. Now get over it!" slipped out of my dry mouth.

"Nothing happened! Mia stop lying and tell her the truth!" he yelled thinking that this was about him.

"I showed you better than I can ever tell you," I continued. "So get over it!"

She swelled up ready to take off my head.

"Get over it!" she yelled. "You thought that Brian wasn't gonna' tell me you fucked him?" she whispered completely ignoring her husband.

Solae wasn't worried about Daniel going anywhere. She was fixated on a man that was just as low down as she was. I envied her security in her marriage because they had no doubts between the two of them. Even though she cheated on him so many times, she knew that he wasn't going anywhere.

"It's your fault. You rang my number the night it happened. What did you expect? For me to pass up a prime opportunity?" I said.

"On top of all of that, you gonna' tell my husband that I'm cheating on him and then had an abortion! You're violated! No one comes and fucks with my money."

"Solae did I do anything differently than what you would do in this case?" I asked.

"Are you fucking serious? You must have some sort of death wish."

Now that she was on the receiving end of getting worked over, she couldn't take it. The misery in her eyes let me know that she wasn't as strong as she pretended to be. I wasn't sorry for anything I did. She pushed me so hard that I fell against a cedar chest. Solae grabbed me by my ponytail, dragging me out of the ground-floor bedroom. Resisting was useless as I was mopped across the black-checkered hallway floor.

"You dirty slut!" she grinded.

Her judgment covered me like a cloud of smoke. It didn't sink in, because this was coming from a cheater. I pulled myself up. While she still had my hair in her fist I swung, hitting her right in the jaw. I wasn't going to let her get the best of me again. Daniel overpowered me forcing me outside. The early morning sun beamed down on me as I laid on the damp ground. Solae stood over me. Looking dead in her eyes, I showed no fear.

"You will neva' have no good luck, so you might as well die bitch!" she cursed me.

Her spit landed in my face and I cringed. This was far from over.

I dialed his number because I needed to vent. Soon after the phone starting ringing I regretted my decision to ask him for anything.

"I don't have any where to go." I told Brian thinking that he would have an ounce of compassion and allow me to live in his vacant apartment in the city.

"Shit happens and then you die, so I suggest you do that." Brian said harshly.

"Please." I begged.

"Don't call here no fucking more."

The phone went dead. I tried to dial out but the message informed me that I no longer had service. Jeremy cut me off. Everything . . . my home, college education, and best foe were gone because of this married man. So far, my dad's predictions were accurate.

"Please not now." I said aloud, banging on the steering wheel. I turned the key in the ignition and stepped on the gas but the engine wouldn't turn over.

"Shit!"

I slammed the door shut and kicked the side of the car, the only thing that I owned out right. I looked up at the sign that said, *Welcome to Harrison County.* My legs were so heavy that it felt like ten-ton boulders were strapped to my ankles. Seven dollars! I laughed hysterically looking through my wallet.

18

This is what my life had been subjected to: a two-bedroom apartment with a pullout sofa, a few basic appliances, and a twenty-seven inch TV, in Crestview Towers which is a low-income project on the north side of town. I stood in the middle of my hellish situation shaking my head because this was my life, until I could climb out of this dark hole.

I laid on the air mattress, wondering what I'd done to deserve such a fate. I didn't get the answer, but what came to mind was the fact that Brian had never given a damn about me, even when I willingly gave up everything for him. I sat up with a new found clarity. My obsession for him to be my man turned into an obsession for him to be a father to my kids. Finally, my obsession turned to revenge. There was no way that I was going to let him continue living a good life in that town house while I was in the projects with nothing. Oh, he was gonna' do right by me if that's the last thing he did.

Brian got my message loud and clear, and he was at my door. It took a child support order for him to show me any kind of respect. He looked like he was going to be sick. His nose was turned up in the air like he was standing in the middle of a dump. There was no need for him to be so uppity because I was in this predicament because of his self-centeredness.

"This place is disgusting." he said standing in the middle of my small, depressing living-room, moving nothing but his eyes.

Brian was sharp, wearing a navy blue linen set with matching gators. As usual, nothing was out of place with his better than everybody attitude. I looked down embarrassed by my second-hand, mint-green sweat suit, decked out with missing studs.

"What do you want Brian? Shouldn't you be with your wife or that bitch you fucked in my kitchen?"

"This visit isn't about anybody but us. Now that I see how common you're living, I can't have no children of mine in no dump like this." he said with a change in attitude.

"What's with the sudden concern for my children? Oh, I get it now. You're only here because of that child support order I put on your ass. Well, you being here won't change my decision. I'm keeping the order because you like to flip-flop like a dead fish. You let me down so much that I can't depend on you to provide on your own."

Instead of sitting down on my itchy, plaid Rent-Rite sofa, he towered over me. There was nothing that he could really say, because I was right about what I had just said. I was just pissed that I didn't think to take this step months earlier.

"Now that you mentioned it, you didn't have to take those drastic measures. I don't need no white man telling me to take care of my children."

"I asked you nicely for help, and you turned me away . . . countless times. You wasn't thinking about these babies when you were treating me like shit, now was you? So don't come in here with your high-and-mighty ass when you have us living in these fucked up conditions, especially while you and your God fearing, submissive wife are living off of scammed money. Shit I want some too!"

"Why are you so mad?" he asked.

"I think you're smart enough not to asked a stupid ass question like that!"

Mad . . . I was beyond mad at this point. Betrayed . . . bitter . . . hurt . . . fuckin' ova it . . . . but not mad. My head was throbbing with so many thoughts. There was too much that I wanted and needed to say about everything, but it wouldn't come out.

"Come on, let me take you to get something to eat, and then I'll take you shopping. Even if you're staying in the projects, this place don't have to look it."

Not only did Brian agree to give me $300 every week, he was going to pay my rent. He thought that I was stupid enough to accept the bare minimum. I was going to play along to get along. I was going to get mine, one way or the other.

I propped up in my new bed draped in a zebra print, listening to the pounding. Brian was snoring hard, and I wanted to leave it that way while things were peaceful between us. I didn't know anyone in this neighborhood so when the knocking got louder I dragged myself to the front door.

"Who is it?"

"You need to tell my husband to come out here now!" Traci yelled through the door.

This was going to be a rare occasion, and I was going to make sure of that. She needed to get used to the fact that this was going to be his second life, whether she like it or not. And since I was in control here, she wasn't welcomed whether her husband was here or not.

"Listen. Get away from my front door, or I'm going to call the cops!" I returned.

"You aren't going to do nothing!" she continued still banging on the door. "Especially when you tricked my husband!"

She had the wrong idea about everything. Instead of choosing to be alone and give up her title to me, she fell for his lies. I turned around, and Brian was fully dressed. I shook my head giving him a laugh of disbelief.

"You need to respect the fact that she's still my wife."

"She need to respect the fact that this is my place, no matter how shitty it is. Have y'all forgot that I'm having your babies!"

"That don't mean nothing! She's more important than you and those babies! The sooner you realize that and accept it, the easier your life will be. Now, I'm going home with my wife. I'll call you when I get a chance."

Brian shut the door behind him leaving me alone . . . again.

19

Brain running back and forth between me and his wife became my new norm. Who wanted to knowingly share their spouse? That's not the life that I wanted to live, but it was better than being alone. Soon I would have my babies to ease some of the pain caused by their father.

I hated Traci because she was in the way. If she wasn't going to leave willingly, then I was going to force her ass out. Last night I slashed all of the tires to her new Jaguar SKE and put shampoo and conditioner in her gas tank. That miserable bitch thinks that she can put me down because she has more than me. The annoying part about it all was that she still wouldn't leave Brian for anything. Every morning I sent her messages reminding her of my place in her husband's bed. But she ignored it as if it was a casual occurrence.

This morning wasn't any different. I sent Traci a video of me and her husband in her bed the day before yesterday. I'd do anything for a little piece of paradise, even ruining lives. But seeing Brian's wife crumble from our relationship was more gratifying than any amount of money especially since she's better than me.

Out of nowhere, a nervous feeling overcame me. I brushed it off as first-time jitters of becoming a new mother. I went into the kitchen and placed the two pieces of potato bread on a plate when someone knocked on the door. My palms got sweaty, and a burst of heat ran through me. My bloated body was positioned in front of the door. I just couldn't bring myself to open it.

I might not have known her name, but I sure as hell remembered her face. There wasn't anything special about her. What stood out to me was her negative attitude towards me which she had for some unknown reason. For the first few months that I'd lived at the Crest, I made it my business to stay to myself because this life was a borrowed one that I intended on giving back ASAP. But I could tell that she wasn't going to make it easy for me to live here.

I recalled the times when I did have contact with her. Indirectly, she made it her mission to comment on my, *stuck-up, conceited ass.* Taking it to a childish level last week, she walked by and bumped me. If she felt like this about me, I couldn't understand what was she doing at my door.

I opened the door just enough to fit me in. The last thing that I wanted was to let her take a look inside my home. I didn't part my dry lips, but my hard stare said everything.

"Um, you don't know me . . ." she started, smacking on her gum.

That was true, and I intended on keeping things that way.

"Anyway. I'm Kera, and I been fuckin' your baby daddy fo' some time now."

My eyes were fixed on the gold-capped tooth, sitting in the front of her big mouth. I heard exactly what she said, but it was surreal to the point that I thought that I was reliving yesterday. She waived her hand in front of my face, getting my attention.

"Did you just say you fuckin' Brian? My children's father?"

"Sho' did." she smacked on her full lips.

I laughed in her face because this shit was funny to me.

"When did all of this go down?" I asked.

That was the first thing that came to mind. Now that I asked the question, I was mad that I was even entertaining bullshit.

"Don't worry 'bout all that. Know that it happened."

"Cool." I said moving out of the door.

What she was trying to do wasn't going to work because it hadn't surprised me. She stuck her thick hand out when I tried to shut the door. Ugh, I didn't feel like dealing with things, but she was.

"Bitch who do you think you are?" she asked.

I took a step back, and examined the intensity of the situation. Kera's full, pear-shaped body was stuck in tight jeans and a white t-shirt. Her visibly overdone face was embellished with lashes that looked like caterpillars. Her neon green glitter eye shadow looked like she was ready to go to the club at three in the afternoon. I would have smacked that smug-ass grin off her face if I wasn't eight months pregnant.

"If you know so much, then I don't need to answer that question."

"Make no mistakes about who you getting smart with. I will trash your ass, pregnant or not, and I'm not gonna' stop fuckin' him! I'd be a damn fool to let him and all of that money go!" Kera snapped.

I wasn't naïve enough to think that any man, including mine, wasn't capable of cheating. The same way you get him is the same way you gonna' lose him. Brian wasn't mine to begin with. He was a male hoe, so I knew what the situation was. It was bad enough that I had to share him with Traci, but now he had added Kera to the extended list. When was too much gonna' be enough?

Brian intentionally choosing a chick from my unit was hurtful. And to select a hood-rat like her was low-budget, even for him. I guess that's the only way he knew how to be. But for the life of me, I couldn't understand why she had the problem with me when she chose to mess with my man. I needed to find out why he chose her.

"Take that shit back to your place and never come back here. I'll fuck you up, baby or no baby!" I yelled in her shocked face.

Brian has given me nothing but ultimatums, requests, suggestions, and forbiddance. He also told me never to come to his church for the purpose of keeping everyone out of his personal life. All of this crazy shit added up to the fact that he wanted nothing but control over my life. It had been his way up until I found out that he was fuckin' my neighbor, so he forfeited my submission and loyalty to him.

There were bright lights and flat screens mounted around the church. Hundreds of shouting voices of the unsuspecting church goers made me dizzy. It saddened me to see that they were being led by a devil. Trying to regroup before I made my next move, I closed my eyes when I heard the sweetest voice in my ear belted out a gospel song. I opened my eyes and Brian, a disguised fraud to some, was standing in the pulpit. It was like night and day. They obviously didn't know him like I did. As I walked down the center aisle towards the front of the church, I ignored every-single eye that was on me and the whispers of ushers trying to seat me. I spotted Traci in her oversized royal-purple sequined hat. She was playing her role. Brian paused for a second when he saw me coming towards him. I shuddered to think of the repercussions I'd have to deal with for going against him again. Oh well, shit happens and then you die. Weren't those his words?

This must have been destiny because the only vacant seat was next to the first lady. I switched up to the front of the church with my over-grown belly. As much as she didn't want to, she kept her dignified composure. I winked at her and smiled warmly. Traci swallowed hard, folding her trembling hands on her silk leg cover as I took my place as *Second Lady of Zion.*

"Today, I would like to talk to you about the repercussions of a lustful and adulteress lifestyle."

"Amen!" the church sung.

I nudged his wife.

"This should be good. I'm going to love being a member of this church." I whispered.

I sat back and crossed my legs.

20

My contractions started at 4:12 a.m. and on Thanksgiving of all days. I laid over the bathtub praying that his pain would end because it was worse than a toothache. It felt like a spiked boulder hitting me in my stomach. Small, shallow breaths escaped my dry mouth as I waited for him to answer his phone. I refused to do this alone because I didn't make these babies alone. So if I had to cross my legs to keep these babies in until I got a hold of him, that is what I was going to do.

"I need to speak to Brian . . ." I said waiting for the last contraction to pass.

The hot sweat rolled down my face, and the pain intensified. My body felt like it was being ripped apart from the inside out. I wanted it to be over.

"Bitch you have some nerve calling my home!" Traci grunted.

"I'm about to have the babies."

"Let me get this straight. After getting pregnant by my husband, you continued to sleep with him. You embarrassed us by coming to our church, causing all kinds of gossip. And you expect me to call him to the phone because you're about to have triplets, his children, the only thing that I haven't been able give him . . ." she ran off.

I could hear the anger that forced its way out of her body. What I also heard was Brian in the background telling her to hang up the phone. To a certain extent, I understood how she felt because she wasn't the only one that was dealt a dirty hand by the Minister. She could hate me all she wanted, but I needed him now. I was going to send him back when I was done, like I did every other time.

"Yes!" I yelled doubled over the bathtub buckling at the knees.

The phone was clutched in my hand so hard that my hand became red and numb.

"Go to hell bitch!" she yelled.

"Hello!"

Traci's hanging up on me wasn't going to change the facts. She needed to get over the fact that her husband was going to be a father and not by her womb. My anger towards Brian and Traci took my mind off the pain. He talked all types of shit about me respecting his wife. He needed to give her that same lecture about respecting me, and my position in his life. In the hopes that he'd answer my call by the time I got to the hospital, I grabbed the overnight bag that I'd packed and headed out the door. This couldn't wait.

Despite the chill in the air, my body was burning up. Childbirth was taking its toll on me and my body. I wasn't understanding why some women did this multiple times. But for me, there was nothing glamorous about what I was going through, alone to bring these babies into the world.

"Fuckin' bitch!" my voice formed rings of smoke in the early morning air.

It couldn't have been anybody but Kera who she slashed my tires, and I didn't have to see her to know that she did it. There was no way that I was going to wait for a cab to take me to the hospital. Memorial Medical Center was nine blocks away, and the only way I was going to get there was if I walked.

I got to the hospital, and it only took me an hour. I was scared to death when my temperature spiked up to 105 degrees, and the doctor told me that I had to get an emergency, c-section. But the most embarrassing part was when they asked who should they call to be by my side. I simply held my head down in shame and whispered,

"If you know where he is, then you'll know more than me."

I stalled and delayed my surgery for as long as I could. I called one more time. While the phone rang in my throbbing ear, I prayed softly.

"Hello." she answered.

I took the phone down and looked at the screen.

"Put Brian on the phone."

Kera huffed hard causing the phone to static.

"Listen boo, Brian is sleep and that's where he goin' to stay. I got your sad ass message 'bout you goin' in labor . . . Who gives a fuck? Listen here sis, you begging' a man to stay 'round is pathetic as hell, so fall the fuck back 'cause the next time I tell you, I'm gonna' beat you the fuck up. So I suggest you call your real baby daddy! Oops, he's dead!" she yelled referring to David.

"Gurl, you lost your damn mind! Put Brian on the phone!"

"Gurl, he ain't payin' you no mind or checking for you! Who do you think showed me the messages? Who do you think told me to answer the phone and handle your dumb ass? Hum?"

"I'm pregnant with his babies, so our conversation shouldn't have gotten this far."

"Bitch, I'm gonna' take it to where I want it to be. So let me make this plain and simple, so even you can understand. Brian ain't fuckin' coming. So go on, and have your bastard babies alone. Leave my man the fuck alone!"

In less than an hour, my world was going to change forever. With the bright-white light hovering over me and the machines around me drowning out my agony, I had to keep reminding myself that it was me against the world, so I prepared myself as I laid on the table to become a single mother. The loud cry of a baby made me sad and lonely. I messed up my own life, and now, if I didn't give up on their father, I was going to mess up their lives too.

"Congratulations Miss Latham, it's a boy! . . . Wait, a baby girl and another girl!" the doctor said.

The nurse that held my hand whispered through her mask.

"He is handsome, and your girls are real life China dolls. What are you going to name them?"

Refusing to look at my children, I kept my head turned towards the nurse.

"Brandon Jeremiah, Miranda Aryee, and Malian Nicole Latham."

What is worst than Brian not showing up is the fact that I had to leave the babies in the hospital. To add to the growing stress is that, I had to hear from Kera that Brian wanted a DNA test. Of course I told them to go to hell and take that damn test with them.

As soon as I entered the NICU, I seen Brain standing over Jeremiah's bed and I smiled. It was immediately wiped off of my face when I got a full view of what was going down. He had the nerve to bring his bitch to see my babies. My heart pounded out of my chest causing me to almost pass out when I saw the nurse swabbing my son's cheeks.

"Are y'all fucking kidding me!" I yelled disregarding the signs that said: *Quiet Please.* "I did not authorize any DNA test and that bitch ain't even family and y'all let her in here to steal my babies! Call security!"

"Please Miss. Latham, you have to keep your voice down. You did name Mr. Abrams as the father, so by law he has the right to request proof of paternity." the doctor said after he rushed over to calm a boiling pot.

I was so mad that I was shaking like an unsteady tree in a hurricane. My words had come back to haunt me. Brian smiled so hard that his face looked like it was going to shatter like cheap glass. He was above the law and this confirmed it for me. He was so cunning that he could get away with anything because he was believable and had money.

"That maybe so, but get your bitch outta' here! Brian, you are so disrespectful!"

This was the first time that I ever saw Kera quiet. I knew the real her and she was ghetto as hell. This was her plan to make me look like the out of control female while she remained calm. I didn't care what they thought about me, especially when it came to my babies.

"That's fine, Kera lets go. I got exactly what I came here for."

I was to my breaking-point with everyone. The day my kids were born, I became determined to take away from Traci what she had taken away from me. Brian should have been there, but because Traci couldn't give him what I had given him, she robbed my kids of their father. I bet that she probably threatened to take his cushy life from him, knowing her husband's weakness, greed. So when he had to make a decision, we loss hands down.

At 3:30 in the morning the temperature dropped considerably. I pulled the hood over my head, being careful not to show my face. There it was lit in pink, *Echelon*. Looking around, I knew I was all alone with no one to stop me. All I could see were the faces of everyone that, in one way or the other, ruined my life. I held the mixture in my hand, and took the lighter out of my pocket. The shattered glass landed at my feet like a million pebbles falling from a sumac tree. I sent a message that couldn't be misinterpreted.

Reporting to you live from downtown Atlanta: Upscale Beauty Salon Echelon Hair Studio has been reduced to rubble when it burnt to the ground in the early morning hours. More details on the six o'clock news.

21

Brian put his arm around my waist, pulling me close to him. His actions surprised me considering that he had chosen to screw some trashy-ass bitch instead of coming to see his kids being born. And when I forced him to explain why he wasn't there he said,

"I didn't feel like sitting in anybody's hospital for any reason. Especially on Thanksgiving."

Today was no different than any other day being in his world. Earlier he spat in my face and told me that he wished that he'd never met me. I knew that this was about image to him, so I refused to take his gesture seriously.

"Unk, this is *one* of my girls Mia."

I gasped at the words *one of his girls.*

"Mia, this is my Uncle, Omar."

This was the first time that I wasn't proud to be labeled his girl. I really thought that my feelings would change once he let our secret relationship be known. Instead, it was empty. I just gave birth to his kids, so I felt entitled to a better label instead of his *side-piece.* Yeah, he upgraded me to one of his, but in hindsight, being associated with him still left me feeling worthless.

Everyone at the Christmas party looked like new money, and I looked like paper food stamps. I felt the stares and whispers as

I solemnly looked down at the jeans, sneakers, and button-down sweater that I had on. To say the least, I was embarrassed and out of place. Tonight, I was going to make myself invisible like Brian insisted many times before. This was the first time that I could admit that I was out of his league and would never fit into his world.

Used to being left out of the special events that he attended, I only saw Brian, if at all, during booty-call hours, so that no one would see us and ruin his reputation. And it was nothing for him to tell me about all the beautiful and successful women that he ran through. At least I knew where he was tonight. Now that I was seeing it first hand, his lavish life took on an entirely different meaning. I wanted to get my babies from my dad and go home.

Omar extended his hand, and I reciprocated. Despite the justified irritation I had towards his nephew, I wouldn't take my hard feelings out on Omar, so I bit my tongue although my insides were on fire.

"Its nice to meet you." I managed.

"You as well. Make yourself at home. Food is in the kitchen, and the bar is in the basement."

"Thank you." I said refusing to look in Brian's direction.

Omar winked at me before turning towards his nephew.

"You sure don't waste no time do you?" he asked with raised eyebrows.

I'm sure Brian knew exactly what he was talking about. Knowing the person that I was dealing with as much as I did, he was only going to let be known what he wanted to be known. I could tell that there was more to their story than what they were letting me know.

"I learned from the best." he replied.

"For sure. So, I don't have to tell you what you already know then? But I'm going to let you know that Ryiann is here."

"I didn't know, but thanks for that information."

"What's the problem? You had to know that she was coming. Ryiann told me that you told her to meet you here at nine. Its nine to be exact."

And here it was: the foolishness. I laughed at the two of them when they looked at me with baffled looks on their equally handsome faces. There was always a method to Brian's madness. Giving him the benefit of the doubt tonight had me feeling like a sucker. This nigga had me here as a decoy to creep with somebody else's woman, because that is what he does.

I could only shake my head because my deceptive heart had me convinced that he was finally going to do right by me and his kids. Yeah . . . this was some more bullshit, at my expense.

Brian dropped me when he heard that she was there. This Ryiann had his nose wide open as he scanned the decorated room for her. Just like everything else that Brian did, I decided to block out the truth.

"Mia, I need you to stop smothering me."

He changed quickly and said,

"Make yourself useful and fix me a plate. And get yourself some salad 'cause you getting a little too chubby for my taste." he insulted.

My eyes pleaded with Brian not to do this to me in front of people. It wasn't enough that he already brought me here looking like a hot mess, but now he was going to finish me off by ripping me to pieces in front of his uncle. What Brian was doing was turning the knife that he'd already forced into my heart. I couldn't handle this, not tonight in addition to postpartum depression.

"Brian, do us all a favor and keep your mouth shut for the rest of the night." Omar said in my defense as I walked away.

Piling barbeque chicken, greens, and potato salad onto his plate, I couldn't keep my eyes off of him or the five-foot-six, blond haired, and ice-blue eyed Barbie that he was happy to stand by. I envied her flawless, coke-bottle figure that was covered in a bronze, backless dress. She was physically pretty thanks to her husbands money. Brain whispered into her ear, and she giggled, throwing her streaked extensions over her bare shoulder. He moved her hair out of her face, and said something else, but this time he kissed her on the neck.

I squinted . . . it was her . . . the one in my kitchen. My heart ached like he put it into a blender and hit puree. Instead of taking him his plate, I took a piece of chicken and ripped the meat clean off of the bone. I didn't know what to do about this situation. What hurt even more was that Brain flaunted their relationship knowing full well what they had done to me.

"I want to apologize for my nephew's behavior."

Turning around with the chicken bone still hanging out of my mouth, I almost jumped out of myself. I shook my head again because I wasn't the only one that knew I was dealing with a low-life bastard. And instead of his uncle apologizing, it should have been Brian.

"I'm okay. I'm used to it." I said pathetically.

"Nephew or not, you deserve better than that. I don't know where he comes from because we aren't like that. He's an arrogant asshole."

Omar placed his hand on my shoulder and gave it a gentle pat. The apple don't fall too far from the rotten family tree, so the only man that I trusted was the one that I gave birth to a month ago. Everyone else that I've come across proved to be untrustworthy. And the one in front of me who was pretending to be concerned could go right to hell along with his nephew.

"You don't need to remind me of anything. I already know who I'm dealing with, and what I got myself into. I can't do anything about that now because we have a kids together."

Omar rubbed his hand over his face which further baffled me because he acted like he didn't know that the kids existed.

"What, so it is true?"

"Yes, they're a month old. Two girls and a boy . . . triplets."

I pulled out my phone and showed him the pictures glowing over what I created.

"Damn! Traci called me days ago hysterical about it. It's sad that she can't have kids. Before they got married, he knew that she was sterile. She had cervical cancer. They agreed that if they wanted kids then they would adopt. But having a woman tell you that she's pregnant by your husband is fucked up, and he is too. It was typical of Brian to pretend that his wife was crazy especially when women would bring kids to her home, job, and church," he sucked his teeth. "He can't deny those," he said looking at my kids. "Yeah, they kin to the bone."

"She ain't crazy 'bout that. Wait . . . how many do he have?"

"Six, including yours. Maybe you can answer this question. Why do y'all deal with him knowing all that y'all know? He's playing with y'all hearts, feelings and emotions. You got: his wife who's trying to live by the Bible by staying married to him, Neiva who believes that she can change him if she stay, Kera the hoe, Ryiann, his bosses' wife, the other ones and you. Look at how he embarrassed you by not telling you the dress code and belittling you in front of me . . . this shit is crazy and y'all are too." he spoke his feelings about the entire chaotic situation.

"What's in it for you? Blood is thicker than water, so why are you going against your blood?" I questioned.

"Because I don't approve of what he is doing. He's been getting away with hurting too many people, and it needs to stop. And besides, I don't want to see you get hurt even more than what you have been."

"Why do you care? You don't know anything about me."

"I know more than you think I do. I know that he don't love you."

I was beyond tired of people telling me things that I didn't want to hear.

"I think it's time for me to go."

I sat the plate down and went into the living room. My only goal was finding Brian and getting the hell out of here. Snakes moved faster than I thought, because I took my eyes off of him for only a second, and he was gone. Whether or not Omar allowed me to, I moved past a few half-dressed women sitting on the cream-plush-covered stairs. Omar's two story single home was beautiful. I rubbed my hands across the cherry-wood fixtures in the hallway before I opened each door and peeked inside. After searching every inch of Omar's house, I realized that Brian had left with his white woman.

The freezing air was my only company as I stood on the front porch. I was hoping that Brian came back before anyone, especially Omar, found out that I was still out there after an hour. The curtains moved behind me and irritated me more than I already was. I refused to look at Omar, so I kept moving back and forth, ignoring him to keep from exploding. I never acknowledged the door when it opened and shut behind me.

"Don't let your pride cause you to get hypothermia. Come inside, get warm, and wait for him to come back. No telling how long his night is gonna' be." Omar said taking a cheap shot.

"No thank you. I'd rather wait out here."

He laughed.

"Suit yourself."

Warm tears rolled down my cold face. Brian treated me like trash because I accepted his behavior. There were many times that I had an out, but I let him back without any accountability. All that I needed right now was to find a way home. I was hurt, but I knew that all Brian needed to do was say the right thing, and he'd slide back in his comfortable position.

When I saw the last person leave Omar's home I swallowed hard and let myself in. He didn't say a word as he rested himself on the arm of the wine-colored sectional. He folded his arms as if he was expecting me.

"I can't seem to break away from him. It's like he's got some sort of hold over me that I can't break." I blurted.

"It's called manipulation baby girl. Sit back, watch and, analyze everything that has happened since you met him. First, he presents himself and makes you believe that he has it all together. He's handsome, successful in his own right, and has a good mouthpiece. And when you spend time with him, he comes across better than most. Brian creates an image which conveys that everyone is lucky to be in his world. You fight to get in and stay in, and then he tears you down mentally until you wake up and realize that years have gone by, and you can't get out."

Knowing that everything that came out of Omar's mouth were facts, my lips parted, and I fell back onto a chair.

"What happened?" I mumbled.

"I don't follow." he said.

My heavy head tilted letting him know that this was the moment of truth. Omar shifted his weight on the chair, blowing a heavy stench of *Taylor's Port* into my direction.

"About ten years ago, I was dating this fine sista' from our church named Gia. Brian had a crush on her for as long as I can remember. But she took the more mature approach, if you know what I mean. I was living high off of life. Baby girl, I had everything I wanted. Coaching junior football was my way of giving back. I had a great job, this house, cars . . . . I was good. The police and league got anonymous calls saying that I was selling drugs and doing other things that I don't even want to mention. The accusations ruined my entire life. I don't have any proof, but deep down in my soul I know that my nephew started that typhoon rolling."

"How do you know it was him?" I asked.

He laughed as if I didn't need to ask questions to the answers that I already knew. Yeah, putting people in jail was his thing.

"Anyway, the cops held me on a forty-eight hour hold. When I got out, I went right to Gia to explain what happened. She pretended that she wasn't home for as long as she could. I wasn't giving up on her, but she wrote me off at the drop of a dime. When she finally came to the door in a see-through gown, she smelled of betrayal, and I knew what it was. I saw my nephew come out of the bathroom in a towel. You can draw your own conclusions from that. He lied to get me out of the picture, so he could move in on what was mine. His plan worked partly. I didn't go to jail, but I lost her. Two days after he used her up, he charged up her credit cards and left her ass high and dry. She tried to come back, but I don't drive backwards. That's the behavior of true blood.

"Omar, why do you have him around, knowing he did all that to you?"

"Baby I'm old school. You keep your friends close and your enemies even closer. That goes the same for family."

22

Suddenly, there was a great need for me to go back to Brian's church. This time, instead of being bold and upfront, I needed to see the full picture so I decided to step back. This was the first time that I laid eyes on Brian since he left me at Omar's party two-weeks ago. If he wasn't going to come to me, then I had to come to him.

Speculator's whispers filled the vestibule as the worshipers hung around the bulletin board. I pushed through the crowd just as nosy as the next and asked,

"What's going on?"

"Minister Abrams just fathered triplets and not by his wife. Its not gossip because its 99.999% facts. If you know what I mean. So the rumors were true, this leader has been living a double life." the sister said shaking her head anticipating spreading the news further.

"What? Did First Lady Traci see this?" I asked, because I wanted her to know that this was my way of rubbing the nasty, forbidden truth in all of their faces.

"Yeah, poor thing. They had to carry her out here on a stretcher this morning."

Sweet revenge.

The crowd was heavy as usual, and Brian had chosen to get bodyguards to protect him from all of the enemies that he'd created. So, even if I wanted to get close to him, I couldn't. I was just satisfied being in the same room with him. I knew that he didn't feel the same way about me, but that's how much I loved him.

After pushing through people that thought that Brian was some sort of super being, I got close enough to see Ryiann and her husband. She smiled so hard at Brian that I thought that her face was going to crack. It was sad watching her husband hold onto her not knowing that he was being cheated on. Our eyes met, and the color drained from her face. She thought I was going to expose her. I could, and I wanted to. But this was too soon. In this case, I would love the element of surprise. When I exposed everything.

Brian caught her eyes and followed them to where I was standing. I could tell that she was panicking as she should have. I couldn't forget how I first met her. I still said nothing as they tried to eye gesture their next move. I wasn't sure what they were saying when Brian shook her husband's hand, and they walked off in a hurry. I completely ignored him when he shook his head no at me like I was a disobedient child. Especially after everything he did to me, nothing that he wanted me to do was going to happen. Instead I focused all of my attention on his mistress.

I disregarded mumbles about my rudeness when I pushed through the crowd. I got outside in time to see the two of them climb into a black Acura Coupe with the license plate *Georgia CRW-1771*. I added to my memory.

It was hard for me to sit by silently and watch Brian and Ryiann's bond become inseparable. What killed my soul is the fact that he didn't mind being seen with her in public. Brian didn't mind spending his money on her, disregarding the fact that I was struggling with his children. But I didn't realize how deep their affair went until I found out that he was willing to risk it all to be with her. I put up with his shit for years and got nothing, and this concept was hard for me to swallow. What was so promising about her?

Ryiann was living comfortably in her condo in suburban Atlanta with her husband, driving her fifty-thousand dollar car, fucking my man, and taking his cash and gifts every chance that she got. She had to go. I rang the bell and waited. If I had to camp out here all night, then that was what I was going to do. I made it my mission to let Eric know who had been in his bed before the night was out. Some people might feel that it was none of my business, but they made it my business when they crossed me.

"Can I help you?" she asked politely like she didn't know me.

That nice shit didn't phase or impress me because she was a whore of a different color. Seeing her up-close, I couldn't understand Brian's fascination with her. Her cratered face was covered heavily with foundation that was two shades lighter than her skin. I understood exactly what type of women Brian was into, fake women. Her blond hair was pinned up, showing a pair of diamond hoops that he bought as an early Christmas gift. When she moved, her olive-green scarf shifted revealing a few passion marks.

"I need to see your husband."

She went pale as a ghost. Riyann shook her head. I bet Eric didn't think that he had a cheating hoe on his hands, but he was going to know today.

"Who are you?" she questioned uncertain of the outcome.

"Listen, you are in no position to question me about anything. But since you wanna' pretend like you don't know me and why I'm here, I need to know why you are fucking my man?" I asked.

Shocked that I chose to confront her about her well-kept secret, Ryiann held her chest. She actually thought that she could have the best of both worlds. It was fine as long as it wasn't with my man.

"Who's your man?" she whispered.

"Oh, so you're a hoe? How many other women's men have you ran through? Brian is so stupid to think that he's the only one." I said not surprised.

"Brian . . ."

A courageous smile came across her face. The fact that she lit up at the mention of his name made it obvious that Brain was something special to her. I shook my head because she wasn't even trying to hide what she was about.

"Yes Brian. I wonder if your husband knows that his employee is counseling you in the bedroom? I doubt it. That's why I'm here to tell to him."

"Why are you trying to ruin my life?" she asked.

I looked at her plush home. What she had was heaven compared to the hell that I was living in. I was fed-up with all these prissy bitches that had everything and thought they were struggling. Ryiann couldn't begin to imagine what I'd been through ever since I met Brian. And if she thought that I was going to move aside and let her in, then she knew nothing. I was going to ruin her life if it was the last thing that I would do.

"When he's spending his money on you, he's not taking care of his kids. I really don't give a fuck about ruining your life or what you talking about. Now where is Eric?"

"He said that they weren't his kids. So whatever you two got going on, leave me out of it." she said still not caring about what he had done to me.

Ryiann actually let that come out of her mouth. She thought that shit was sweet now. Once Brian got tired of her, and she served no purpose to him, Ryiann would skin her fake ass after he threw her out on the sidewalk. And as usual, I was going to be right there watching the entire scene play out. I seen them come and go.

"Bitch you don't know shit! Enough said. Let's see what your husband has to say."

I turned around to walk away when she grabbed my arm. I snatched it away.

"Wait, you don't have to do that. I didn't know about you? The way he explained things, you were a stalker just trying to get some money."

"Don't lie. You knew me when you was disrespecting my house! So stop making me think that I'm crazy!" I yelled in her face.

"What can I do to make this go away?" she pleaded.

People with money always thought that there was a price attached. No amount of money would give back what she took from me. I was done with the idle compromise I was having with her. Then again . . .

"Go get your checkbook." I said seriously.

It was going to cost Ryiann to keep my mouth shut for a little while. After she wrote me a check for five-hundred dollars, I ripped it up in her face. Quickly, she got the message that I wasn't joking. She wrote another one out for fifteen-hundred dollars. I'm sure it didn't put a dent in her Coach wallet. I was certain that Brian was going to give it back to her in more ways than one.

23

"My life is falling apart." Brian said letting out a deep breath and holding his head.

I turned the page of my magazine, uninterested in what he was saying.

"What does that have to do with me?" I asked.

"Traci left me. She served me with divorce papers. I can't risk that because it's cheaper to keep her. That greedy bitch will get half of everything I own." he said plotting against the woman he wanted to stay married to.

I laughed because now she was a bitch.

"You haven't learned anything . . . you are so selfish and think that everything is always about you or some damn money!" I snapped. "Listen, I hated sharing you with her. There is no doubt about that. But now that she is gone, am I suppose to be sad? I'm definitely not sad because she's about to fuck you over, like you did me. So you can take your pity party somewhere else because I'm not interested in joining you!"

It felt good to get some of these feelings off of my chest, and from the look on his face he got my message.

"What's that right there?" he asked.

Typical Brian had his chest stuck out like he'd done something big. The few presents and toys that he'd gotten for me and the kids weren't shit compared to what he was giving all his other women. I wasn't impressed and I wanted him to leave.

"Not much considering your kids been on this earth for two months, and you ain't done shit for them."

"What's that?" he asked again.

He pointed again at the same measly gifts.

"Big deal Brian! They need food and pampers everyday. You just here because shit is going wrong for you."

"Anyway, I can't sit here and debate this. My life is in turmoil. I need a favor." he said.

All of Brian's: sneaking, lying and conniving, stealing, using, and abusing was aging him. He was pitiful, unattractive and boring. On top of that, once I expose him, he's going to be reduced to nothing.

"Never mind, I'll go to someone who really cares about me and not what they can get out of me."

I laughed at his sad attempt at manipulation.

"With Ryiann? Oh well, since your mood is already messed up, I need to tell you that I had a chat with her." I said never taking my eyes off of the article.

"Mia are you crazy! You know what could happen if . . ."

"Her husband finds out? Yes, I know and let's say that we have an understanding to keep it on a need-to-know basis. Now, I know you have a lot to lose: your job, your position in the church . . ."

"So you gonna' do this to me! You ain't right!" he yelled in my face.

"Shut the fuck up, and keep your mouth closed. You are gonna' do what I say, when I say, and how I say. If you don't want your congregation or boss to know you been fucking his wife."

"Mia baby, please." he begged on his hands and knees.

Seeing him fidget at my feet like the suffering dog that he was proved to be bittersweet. He began kissing me all over, heading to my bare thighs when I lifted his head.

"The dick won't do this time. I'll call you if and when I want it. Now, if you don't mind . . ." I told him.

"I can stay the night and make dinner, and we can decorate the house . . ." he interrupted.

I laughed because this entire scenario was funny as hell to me. Now that I had something on him, he wanted to be the family man that I'd needed from day one. In order for me to keep his secret, he was going to pay a heavy price.

"I'll pass. I'm expecting company, and it wouldn't look right if you were here."

He didn't move when I got off the couch. His eyes never left me as I went to the door and opened it.

"Pick me up tomorrow around two. I need to go shopping, but in the meantime, I want some money." I said with my hand out.

He gave it up without an argument.

I knew that you could never turn your back on the devil. I got all of his calls and messages forwarded to my phone. Brain didn't let a damn thing go. After I got tired of seeing messages from Solae, Ryiann, and a few dozen other women, I had to show him that I wasn't joking.

Solae was so stupid. As much misery as she caused to so many people like me, she should have known that her shit was going to come back to screw her over. Although I hadn't seen her since she kicked me out of her life, she was still up to the same games and being a predictable hoe. I watched her when she parked her car in front of a row of town houses outside of her district. Smiling ear to ear, she jumped from her car and climbed into a silver Bentley. Her text messages were a contradiction. She wasn't actually giving Brian the time of day since she found another golden goose in the form of a young Asian guy.

I still had a spare key to Solae's car from the time I took her kids to their doctor's appointment. From the tracker I downloaded on Brian's phone, I was going to know where he and Ryiann were going to be tonight. I sat outside of a Thai restaurant and waited. I had time to reconsider what I was about to do, but why should I? They deserved their just desserts.

It was dark, and the windows were tinted. I had to squint to see exactly where they were going. Brian couldn't keep his eyes or hands off Riyann. I don't know why, but it still hurt to see them together as if it was the first time I caught them together. This was deeper than sex. If I had to put my money on it, I would say that this was the only woman he was ever in love with.

That thought kept me from staying rational. They were crossing the street when the speedometer reached sixty-five mph. They didn't even see it coming. I swerved to miss him, and the car jerked as if I ran over an imperfection in the road. Watching from a distance, I saw Brian kneeling by her side, and people gathering around them looking up the street. My adrenaline calmed when I parked the car where I found it. I disappeared into the darkness.

It looked like he'd been crying just before he got here. I watched the late-night news where they described the car and gave a partial-license plate of the hit and run. I did what I had to when I called the tip-line and gave them information on my former best friend.

"What's the matter with you?"

"There was an accident, and Ryiann was hit. The driver sped off . . ."

He sniffed.

"Well, I guess karma paid her a visit she couldn't handle."

"That's so mean. Don't you have a heart?"

"Not when the person that got hurt was in my house unwelcome."

"That was the past, but she still didn't deserve to be ran down like a dog."

"If you want me to be hysterical and sympathize, I'm not going to."

"You are so sad." he informed me.

"Actually I'm fine with that. But with all that happened, why are you here, instead of with her?"

"Because I fled the scene. I couldn't risk her husband finding out that I'd been banging his wife for two years."

"And you call me mean."

Brian broke down right before my eyes. I blocked it out and continued painting my toes. Now he knew how it felt to lose something that you loved to death.

Ryiann's hit and run left her in stable condition. She suffered from two broken legs. Solae was arrested for something she didn't do and I was fine with it. I take it anyway I could get it. The situation was settled. Now that they were both out of the way, Brian was finally going to love me.

24

I'm glad that I didn't turndown Omar when he asked to see me again. Some people might think its nasty to deal with two family members, but I don't think that there's any difference between that and what Brain did to me. Brian gets no love, especially now that everything good was happening to me. I'm going to enjoy every second with his uncle.

Omar was amazing me with his gentle, laid-back nature. I don't know what the hell happened to his nephew because they were like night and day. He stood at the stove preparing a lobster and scallop stir-fry. I smiled because Brian probably thought that I was home waiting for him like a creature of habit. If only he knew what was about to go down.

He fixed two plates and sat them on the table and he poured two glasses of white wine.

"I hope you like it."

"I'm sure that I will. I was happy when you called." I said.

"I was alone and thought of you. I couldn't think of a better person to spend my time with."

Its been a long time since someone told me that they wanted me around them. That's when I remembered David. I didn't want to become depressed, so I pushed him in the furthest part of my mind. I knew that all men had their shit with them, but I was loving my new change in pace. But how long was this going to last?

There was a possibility that when Omar got what he wanted, he would change faces like his nephew. I had to pull back before I got in too deep.

"Wait, this is moving too fast. Maybe if I hadn't met Brian first, then I would have been flattered. But I can't do this to myself."

"Babe, stop thinking so hard, and let it flow."

"What about Brian?"

"What about you and what you need? Not only can I provide you with a stable life, but I can make you happy. I'm not a perfect man, but I will be perfect for you."

"I've been promised that before." I said with a sudden sadness.

"But I'll be the first to make it true." he said with confidence.

He got up from the kitchen table. What was he trynna' do to me? Omar knew that this was a line that should never be crossed, but here we were. He sat the blue Tiffany & Co. box in front of me.

"I didn't get you anything." I said feeling bad.

"We'll have plenty of time for that."

Nervously, I fumbled with the silver bow to unwrap the box. My eyes never left the sterling silver bangles. It was crazy how I had put all my heart and soul into a man that didn't give me the time of day and now this. Tonight, I was letting go all of my doubts, fears, insecurities, and letting it flow. I took Omar by the hand and lead him to my bedroom. It was quiet when I sat him on the edge of the bed. It just felt right.

Every since me and Omar made love on Christmas Eve, I had no intentions of contacting him again. There was no need for me to get too close and risk losing again. From the start, everything in my life was chaotic, and he was too good of a person to get hurt by my bullshit. I wanted the good memories of what happened to stay that way. Besides, there wasn't any room in my life for love, especially when there was money to be made. Now, I needed to let go of what might or might not have happened between us.

The New Year was going to bring my life a lot of possibilities because it was now all in my hands. After my new furniture was delivered, Brian handed me his signed divorce papers.

"Are you serious?" I asked.

"Yes, I see things differently now. You always have my back even when I don't treat you right."

Who in the hell was this? It was Brian's body, but his entire mindset was different. I needed this welcomed change of events in my life. But the real question was: how long was this change going to last?

"This is half the battle, but what about the other ones?" I asked.

"They are all gone. I had to get rid of them. They were only good for one thing. Besides, that baby that Neiva was carrying wasn't mine," he said with his head held down. "We got a DNA test."

"Is that so? You just finding that out. I tried to tell you."

"I know I had to learn the hard way. There is something that you don't know . . ."

"What's that?"

"Kera is a nasty thieving bitch!"

"Get the hell outta' here!" I said sarcastically.

Brian knew the game and how it was played, so when he took up with a nasty hood-rat what was he expecting . . . . quality?

"Last night, I went to her place to tell her it was over. She had some dude there. I wasn't impressed about that. I needed the two-thousand dollars back that she stole from my bank account."

He was so materialistic that it made me sick to my stomach. Here it was. I lost almost everything, and he was bitching about a few thousand that he didn't earn.

"What do you expect me to say? If I know one thing, you get what you deserve." I said honestly.

"I know, and I realize that now. I just want to be a family. Me you and our kids."

"I don't know." I said skeptically.

Right where I sat, Brian forced my legs open. I resisted twice. I wasn't going to be a rebound. He was now begging that we become a family, but the idea didn't interest me like it used to.

"Just relax . . . trust me." he said.

I made it a habit not to trust a person that said "trust me."

I opened my eyes to find myself alone. Brian's last statement to trust him floated around in my cluttered mind. What I fought for was finally offered to me, and I didn't want it anymore. I wonder if I ever wanted him or if I wanted him because someone else had him? I didn't have time to debate this dead subject. All I needed was some retail therapy.

"Bitch you think you special?"

This is what I tried to avoid. The only way to deal with Kera was to ignore her, and that is what I intended on doing. Kera continued blocking me from getting into the complex. Whenever she had something on her chest, she needed it to get off before she left me alone. I rolled my eyes because I was over her drama.

The winter darkness allowed me to see only what was right in front of my face. Something had Kera visibly upset to the point that she was ready for a throw-down. Nothing had changed except for the fact that the man we were sharing left her to be with me exclusively.

"Listen to this. We have nothing to talk about because Brian made his choice. Now if you have an issue you need to talk to him."

"No bitch! I wanna talk to you! I don't know what he's been telling you . . ."

"He dumped you and now you're mad . . . I get it!" I yelled.

I was annoyed at the fact that I was dignifying her with any answers.

She reached in the pocket of her leather jacket. I stepped back wishing I had my blade on me. When she pulled out her phone, I knew this could be worse than her pulling a weapon.

"You're so fucking dumb! Does this look like he dumped me?" her voice echoed in the cold air.

Everything was right in my face. I focused on pictures of him and her in my bed yesterday while I was out spending his money. And he had my kids in the middle of his nastiness.

"And F.Y.I, we're moving out of state. That tells you how much he loves you."

My conscience wouldn't allow Traci to leave my head. Or everything that I did to her to get Brian. It was all backfiring in my face. I've been presented with the truth so many times, and I ignored it for the fear of becoming a victim and being alone. I thought I had control of this crazy saga, but that was far from the truth.

What Kera told me New Year's night was obviously the truth because I hadn't heard a word from Brian in eight weeks. The messed-up part about everything was that I was broke, alone, and stuck with three kids. These were all things I dreaded the most.

I assumed that Brian was gone for good and it finally sunk in. I cried because I'd wasted part of my life on nothing. He wasn't laying in bed depressed over me. I had to do something to get me out of the grave I dug for myself.

Omar squeezed me tight and wouldn't let go. I needed that hug because I hadn't felt a real touch since the night I cut ties with him for no apparent reason. I forced myself to pull away because I didn't know how long I could fight back the tears. He stepped back examining me.

"When you called me I was surprised." he said with his normal soothing voice.

"I know. I'm sorry that it took me so long to get back to you . . . I just had to sort some things out."

I didn't want to say that I needed to get Brian out of my system, but that was only true after he left me.

"I'm glad that you called no matter how long it took."

It didn't feel as good as it should have. In my own way, I was treating Omar how Brian treated me. It was unintentional, but I'm sure it hurt the same.

"I owe you a huge apology." I whispered.

"For what?" he asked sitting on the sofa and patting the cushion next to him. I sat down.

"For treating you so damn bad after that night we spent together. If you're okay with the fact that I been with your nephew and still willing to spend your life with me . . . then I'm willing to give us a chance."

SUMMER 2013

25

The dimmed summer's moonlight shined through my bedroom's white lace curtains. I stood in the mirror, staring at myself and trying to trigger my memory as I did many times before. With my mind blank, I focused, hoping that she would come to me in any form. The things that came to me was the fact that Brian never realized that I held his life in the palm of my hands and the last time I laid eyes on my mom. I quickly dismissed Brain as being a major factor in my life to focus on more important things.

I remembered that I was cupped in my father's arm, looking down at her in her white casket. She had a soft smile on her face, and her hands were folded across her long ivory dress. I reached out to touch her, but she: didn't move, didn't respond, and never came home with me.

I was four when it happened, but to me it felt just like yesterday. Sadly, that's all I remember about her. But the many stories that I have heard about my mother were through other people's memories. I often heard that Melani, my mom, was beautiful. Her five-foot-six, curvaceous statue was accentuated with copper skin, light brown eyes, and short curly hair. She was exotic, pure Moroccan and African-American. But her beauty didn't quiet the low whispers of her demons: men and liquor. Associated with her stigma came people and their judgmental tendencies. They tainted her reputation which made everyone that known her forget that she was a successful RN who sacrificed everything for us. Although she wasn't perfect, my mom, didn't deserve to be betrayed by the only man she'd love.

My flowered, terry-cloth robe fell to my ankles. I rubbed my hand over the scarred skin on my lower body that serves as a constant reminder of what is said to have happened that April afternoon. I couldn't imagine the guilt that she felt for marking me for the rest of my life. I cringe at the fact that thirty-percent of my body was burned when my mother accidentally left me in a bathtub of scalding water, as a result of her *drunken blackouts*. Many assumptions followed, and after eleven years of marriage my father left, taking me with him and forgetting his vows: for better or worst. Little did he know, the worst was yet to come.

Six weeks later when we got back to Sugar Hill, we were greeted by Sheriffs and the coroner . . . *she was dead*. On April 25,1990, I felt like my life ended. I never doubt that she didn't love me or daddy, but her demons were bigger than her love for us. Some days I resent him because if he didn't force her hand, then I think she'd still be here with us today. Now, even as an adult, I can't remember anything about her: her touch, her smile, how she smelled, or even how she sounded. It was like she never existed. I can't accept what I didn't know, and that's how I live my life.

I wonder if she ever felt unloved, unappreciated and used? I wonder if she lived the life that she wanted? But for me, it wasn't suppose to be like this. I'm not suppose to be a mother of three at the age of twenty-six, living in a cramped two bedroom apartment in the projects. No job, no career, no money, no purpose . . . nothing. Now that I have been through the unimaginable, I look at things differently as if the scales were finally removed from my eyes while I slept. My life is fucked up, and after five years I made peace with that fact.

What is all of this for? I have a man that will never leave his wife. The fact that he is still cheating on me with that ratchet-ass chick that lives in my complex drives me insane. Brian only takes care of his children when it is convenient for him. He chose to make my life a living hell despite all that I continue to do for him. Constantly, he reminds me that he will never commit to me because *he wanted to keep his options open*. It is heartbreaking. His words echoed through my mind and each syllable tore me down, but I refuse to give up on him. Why do I stay? Who the hell knows. This is my life as I live and breath. *I want out.*

26

In my twenty-six years, I've been through a lot and experienced even more. I chose to sleep with my ex-best friend's boyfriend, took him from his wife, eliminated the competition when it got too hot, and ruined lives when it benefited me. As a result, karma has made me homeless, lonely, broke, miserable, and gave me a man that refused to love me and take care of his responsibilities. Even then I don't think that I'd ever been this low.

My eyes were hopelessly fixed on my children. They sat around the empty glass table while I forced my attention back to the refrigerator that held: baking soda, a few rotten grapes, two heals of stale bread, a swallow of milk, and a quarter stick of butter. Seeing this broke my heart even more than Brian's personal attacks on me. I turned my face again because I couldn't bear to see the pain in their eyes despite the smiles on their faces. I shouldn't have to take care of them alone knowing that their no-good father was eating as he damn well pleased. The image of him flaunting his whore around town giving her anything she asked for pissed me off even more. I now regretted hesitating the other night.

There was only enough buttered rice for my kids to eat and take away their hunger. I wiped my eyes watching how they treated food like a luxury. I had to do something, so I left them alone and took the stairs to apartment 131. All that was on my mind were my kids, and what they didn't have. I pounded on the door, waiting for her to come out. I hadn't heard from Brian in over a week, so I took a wild guess that this is where he might be. It was nothing for him to spend time with her less than 100 feet away from us and not bother to check to see if we were okay. Brian always said that I had to respect his wife, but he didn't say that rule applied to his side bitch.

My ear was suctioned to the door. I knew about her for just as many years as we'd been together, so nothing shocked me at this point. I banged harder and waited. My anger wasn't released because they weren't there. I headed back up to the apartment.

"What else could go wrong?" I said sucking my teeth and playing with the switch.

I headed towards the TV and pushed the buttons, but the screen was still blank. Brian did it to me again. Last month he got my water turned off when I couldn't buy him the same exact *Rolex* that he already had, and now it was the electric.

"Damn!" I cursed still playing with the lights that wouldn't come on.

I had to laugh to keep from crying. The proposition that I'd gotten the past year came to mind. This was a sure way to get out of this black hole and take care of my kids. All I knew was that, I couldn't do this anymore.

"Hello." I yelled into the phone.

"Yeah." he responded casually.

"Yeah? Brian where are you? I have no food for our kids, and my electric is cut off!"

"It was your idea to have them kids. I never wanted them, so taking the responsibility of feeding them is all on you. And to answer your question, I'm in Cancun with Kera. I got the electric cut off because Kera told me how you be having niggas running in and out. Tell them to pay your bills. I'm over this shit and you! Now you wonder why I left you so many times before . . ." he said letting out a condescending laugh.

I thought back to the thirty-nine times throughout the five years of us being together that Brian left and came back. It hurt, but after the fifth time I got used to him treating our relationship like a revolving door. And each time I rolled out the welcome mat for him to dog me all over again.

"I showed you so many times that I don't want you. You just don't give up!"

"Brian, I can't believe that you are being so fucking stupid. It's crazy to believe a hoe like that over me! I hope the pussy is worth your family!"

"Actually, it's better!" he admitted.

I've been in this place too many times before. I was immune to his nastiness, so it went into one ear and out the other.

"This is crazy! You need to ask her how many dudes she be having down there! Dumbass, you not the only one! You are a sorry excuse for a man to allow another bitch to dictate to you how much you do for your children. Its pathetic!" I screamed. "And what did I get for buying you that custom-diamond bracelet? Not a damn thing! Now my babies are hungry because you promised to give me some money, and lied yet again! You know what Brian, you are better off dead to us!" I revealed.

"It was either feed them or buy Kera a few things for our trip. I couldn't have my lady looking bad because that's a reflection on me. You can say whatever you want Mia, but Kera is the best thing that ever happened to me. She's just a little misguided, but I love her unconditionally. And in response to your little comment, the feeling is mutual. My life will be much happier if you'd die." he confirmed his true feelings.

"You must be out of your mind! She's a whore! You know damn good and well that you can't turn a hoe into a housewife!" I yelled forgetting that my kids were still in the room. "And I don't have to be dead to leave your tired ass alone!"

"Jealousy is not a good look for you. Please, do me a favor, leave me the hell alone!"

"Neither is my kids going to bed hungry."

"Well, I suggest you focus your attention on that rather than chasing after me."

Brian was silent.

"Hello . . . hello."

He hung up on me. Like every other argument, it left me drained in more ways than one. I slid to the floor when Jeremiah came to comfort me like many other times. He wiped my tears away with the back of his sleeve. It shouldn't have went down like this, but I couldn't force Brian to be a father when it was obvious that he didn't want to be.

"Mommy, don't cry."

"I'm okay." I said minimizing the seriousness of this situation.

"I'll take care of you and won't ever make you cry."

"I know that's why I love you so much. And I promise I will make things better for you and your sisters."

He hugged me tight, kissed me on my cheek, and grabbed his sisters taking them into their bedroom. I keep telling myself that they were better off without me. Stressing over their father distracted me from being a mother. What else is there for me to do?

This was enough. Silently I made a vow to myself that from this day I wasn't going to cry over anything or anyone. I was going to do it to them before they did it to me. I smiled remembering all I'd gained as a younger, cold-hearted bitch. I needed to revisit that past one more time for the sake of my children.

I viewed Omar like I did any other benefactor. I knew his worth so he wasn't going to get it as bad as any other dude that I was going to run the game on.

"It's Mia . . . do you want to see me? Cool, but stop by the store and bring us some groceries, and make sure you have snacks for the kids." I demanded.

"Give me an hour." he responded hanging up quickly thereafter.

Omar hadn't changed since I met him. Over the years he had become my rock and support in many different ways. It was either black or white with him, and that's why I loved him more than his trifling nephew. We tried the relationship thing years ago, but it just didn't work because he wasn't Brian. When I laid eyes on him this time, it was different. I knew it all along, but finally could admit it. I made the biggest mistake of my life.

This wasn't his obligation, yet without hesitation he just did what a man is suppose to do. He arrived with bags from the meat district, produce junction, Costco, and the toy store. Omar kissed me on my forehead and went to the kitchen. With his back turned he spoke.

"I can see that no good nephew of mine is still up to his same games . . ." he said referring to the empty refrigerator.

A response wasn't needed because the proof was right in front of him. The only good thing about my situation with Brian was the fact that I never needed to tell anyone how he was. He always managed to tell the entire story without opening his mouth. I hunched my shoulders.

"That's because he's in Cancun with his hoe." I said nonchalantly.

There were no secrets between the two of us because Omar knew everything. I knew exactly how he felt about me, and he *understood* why I chose to stay where I was. And he never judged me for that either. So anytime he had something to tell me that pertained to my messed-up-situation, it came across unintentionally hard. He shook his head.

"That shit doesn't surprise me."

"He got the electric cut off because Kera told him some bullshit lies about me having dudes here. That's not true though." I said folding the brown bags.

I looked outside at the setting sun that was softening over the city. The room was darkening, but I was still able to see him which made me smile.

"That coming from a whore," he laughed. "In all seriousness, if a man keeps accusing you of cheating, the likelihood is that he's doing exactly that. And as far as Kera is concerned, a dude that goes to my barbershop knows her if you know what I mean. You know she pregnant?" Omar asked eying the old grapes with his nose turned up.

He was speaking but the last comment wasn't sinking in. My nerves were in the pit of my stomach making me sick.

"What!"

"Yeah. Brian thinks it's his . . . . dumb ass . . . . but Rasheen knows it's his. Karma is a ugly bitch that came in the form of Kera."

"This shit is crazy. He's not taking care of the ones that he has with me, but he claiming that one." I said in disbelief and then remembered who we were talking about.

"Take my credit card and get some lights on. I can't have y'all living like this. I told you so many times to move in with me."

"I know. I just don't want to put that burden on you."

"If I didn't want it, I wouldn't have offered you the perfect way out."

Although I heard this countless times before, this time his offer brought tears to my eyes. I couldn't get pass what he had said. So, this offer was now considerable. My heart told me that Omar was over the games and juggling women. Maybe this is what I needed get over Brian, but I knew that this wouldn't be a long-term solution. I loved Omar, but I wasn't in love with him and that was the difference.

I grabbed him by the hand and took him to my bedroom. This wasn't the first time that we'd been here, but it had been a long time. I was numb from the years of neglect. I was sure that I was fully capable of enjoying this experience. Locking the door behind me, Omar touched my face as if I was too good to be true. Things had never wavered with him making it easy to be me and not who Brian thought I should be. Omar embraced that concept.

His kisses tickled my body until he pulled away. I stood awkwardly as he walked across the bedroom floor. He opened the curtains exposing everything that I was ashamed of. I tried to cover my body with my pants when he snatched the sea-green material from my tight grip. He winked at me in approval of what he saw. This time he kissed my skin tags something that no one had ever done before.

"I love you Mia. I can give you and the kids a better life than my nephew can ever give you. Just give me a chance."

27

"Why do you put up with his shit! Girl, you deserve so much better than that bullshit he's putting you through. I can't for the life of me understand what kind of hold he have on you that would allow you to sell your soul to the devil and still have nothing."

I listened to what Aja said without responding. It was too embarrassing and degrading for anybody to know how I lived and what my children were being subjected to. No woman wanted to admit that she allowed a man to use her without any benefits whatsoever. It was just stupidity. But even if I chose to remain silent about the things that were happening in my life, she would know every detail without me even saying a word.

"I put up with it for five years. I don't know how to get out. Truth be told, I'm scared to be alone. Besides, I invested too much in him to just walk away now without nothing. But I know that no matter how bad Brian treats me, we'll always have our kids who links us together forever."

"Girl cut the Young and the Restless bullshit! This is 2013. It's reality, not fantasy. Brian is dead wrong for the shit he do, but you're to blame too. You knew what he was about, and you didn't do shit. Now you all sad and miserable that he run off on you for the hundredth time since y'all been together. Boo, I love you, but he don't want you, and he never did. All he wanted from you was the ass and not the commitment. And you still gave your heart freely knowing this. Question is, what are you gonna' do?" she asked with curiosity.

In the beginning I got a lot of sympathy, but Aja was over it now. The facts were killing me and it was showing. I looked at my kids that were playing without a care in the world. This was a sad situation.

"I'll do anything that I have to do to make them happy."

"I told you that I can put you down with my job over a year ago."

I contemplated her proposal more than one time. I wasn't in any position to keep turning down easy money. It wasn't like I was a stranger to the hustle, but taking my clothes off in front of strange men wasn't sitting with me. But I had to do something since Brian didn't care. I had to base my decision on what was right in front of me, and leave my emotions out of the equation.

At the age of twenty-eight, Aja Carrington used stripping to earn a master's in public health. She was a single mother who lived in a three-bedroom house in a nice neighborhood. I knew that I could have the same things if I'd stop focusing on the *what-ifs*. You can't help a person that didn't want to be helped, and that's where I was two years ago when she came into my life. I was ready for this now that I didn't have anything else to lose.

"You did, but I was a putting my everything into Brian . . ."

"Fuck Brian!" she said pointing to my kids before she spoke again. "That's your priority right there. Not that nigga, any bitch or situation shouldn't change that. When I swing around that pole seven days a week, or deal with them nasty ass men touching me, its not because I like it. I hate it, but I pretend to love what I do because I do it for them." she said with conviction referring to her kids.

There was no doubt in my mind that Aja wasn't serious about what she was saying. Just like anything else she did, it never went wrong, so I knew that this time wasn't going to be any different. My mind was made up, and I wasn't changing it for any reason.

Tucked away on a desolate strip in the *Bluff*, sat a converted warehouse that was my current situation. The flickering neon lights forced me to shield my eyes as we walked through the graveled lot. The piercing whistles from a few strays without the slightest clue as to what I was up against unnerved me. They threw a few nasty slurs our way letting me know that this was what I had to look forward to. The massive steel door slammed behind us when butterflies decided to take residence in my stomach. I stood next to Aja's side. There was no turning back now that Hakee, the owner of the club, was looking me over like I was new meat on a slab. The stench of sin filled the air. I swallowed it because I just sealed my fate.

"Y'all sista's?" he asked in a Middle Eastern tongue.

We looked at each other for verification. I know that everyone is said to have a twin somewhere in the world, but mine happened to be in the same city and state. Aja's good genes had her looking like she was in her late teens. Her petite height was elevated by the six-inch red-leather, peep-toe boots. She was attractive with silk-like copper skin, light-brown eyes that reflected a hint of green when the sun hit them, and long honey-blond hair.

"Yes we are Hakee. So you gonna' put her on for me?" she asked turning on the charm and rubbing his aging face.

He grinned as the music thumped in my pounding ears, I kept silent.

"You know what that does to me," he said to her. "All new girls go on first. You on in twenty." he told me still enjoying Aja's false attention.

"I sure do boo."

He focused his attention on her again.

"I need to see you in my office after you set her up."

Aja grabbed my hand. She led me pass the bathrooms into a narrow dressing room full of girls, costumes, makeup and chatty gossip. My tired puffy eyes moved but nothing else did. Everything in this musty room sparkled like worthless silverware and these chicks had the nerve to turn their noses up at me like I was a plastic spoon.

"See, I told you I got your back," she said sitting me on an empty stool. "Some rules for you. Nobody here is your friend. Get your money and get out."

"Did I get you in trouble with him? Why do Hakee want to see you in his office?" I asked trying to make idol gossip to take my mind off of my choice.

"That's nothing for you to worry about. When you have a mission, you'll do anything to fulfill that." she said leaving me confused.

I looked over my shoulder because all eyes were still on me. They could tell that I wasn't from the Bluff, and I didn't want to be. I heard stories about the ratchet females down here and I experienced one first-hand, Kera, so I wasn't trying go there with any of these dancers.

"And your business is your business." she continued talking directly into my face as she put fuchsia-glitter-eye shadow on my eyes.

I shook my head. I didn't have to be in the game to know the game. This was about the money, and that was my mindset.

"I got you sis. And thanks for everything," I said.

"It's time. Remember everything I taught you. Sell the fantasy."

I was so glad that I couldn't see anybody in the crowd because if I had, my children would have went hungry again. The lights blinded me and the music and introduction of *Egypt* vibrated throughout my sold soul.

Tonight I wanna dance for you . . . played throughout the Orchid. This was my time to prove to everyone who I was and how I did things. I remembered and envisioned every move Aja demonstrated for me earlier today. It was obviously working because the money and roars from the men confirmed it. I never dreamed that I would be on somebody's stage. Life is so unpredictable.

"You did the damn thing! You heard them out there? It was all for you!" she said hugging me so tight that she was cutting off my already-limited air.

My heart was still racing from the taboo experience. While she glowed like a proud mother I counted my money.

"Three hundred and fifty-two dollars in twenty minutes!"

"Shish, that's not bad for the first spot, and you're new. You know Hakee give all his girls a base pay of a hundred-and-fifty a week and some girls do the VIP rooms."

"Really?"

I focused all of my attention on her.

"Yup."

"What do you do?" I asked.

"Watch and learn."

His eyes followed me all around the club making me a little uncomfortable. Without trying to be obvious like he was, I was wracking my brain trying to figure out if I knew him and if I did, from where. I wasn't the bold type to go and approach him, so I waited for him to come to me for two-and-a-half hours.

The light tap on my bare shoulder took my focus off of him. The light-skinned guy smiled, holding onto a cup and a black-and-mild cigar. Before he said anything he blew three rings of smoke into the already smoky air.

"My friend wants to talk to you."

He pointed to the shy guy sitting in the corner of the crowded room.

"Does this friend have a name? And why couldn't he come and approach me himself? I don't bite."

"Maybe that's what he needs," he laughed. "It's his first time at a strip club. He's not familiar like me."

"I'm sure he's not." I said sarcastically.

"He's Naieem and I'm Meir."

"Cool, let's go see what he really wants from me."

Meir stayed close by my side as I stood in front of Naieem with my hands on my hip. While the wild lights bounced off the walls I tried to get a full view of his face. Naieem was okay, but I was more concerned about how much bank he was working with. Tonight I watched and learned how Aja did things, but what I was going to do was add my twist to what she had taught me to get more.

"Did you have a message for me?" I spoke directly into his ear.

He smiled at my breasts which were in his face.

"I . . . I . . ."

"Just come with me."

I grabbed his hand leading him into a private room.

28

Old habits die hard now that I was coming up. I'm infatuated with money to the extent that it is leading my life. Just having enough of it wasn't satisfying me. I wanted even more. I know what it feels like to be hungry and broke now that I'm passed that phase, I'll do whatever I have to do to keep from going back to the gutter.

The phone rang and I debated whether or not I was going to answer. Lately I been having this nagging feeling not only to keep Aja out of my business, but to keep my distance from her as well. So when she hung up and called back I picked up.

"Wassup boo?"

"You tell me. I saw you and Hasa sneaking out of the club last night. Wassup with that?"

I sucked my teeth because I was going to take her advice. I was keeping my business just that. I pulled down the sun visor touching up my gloss in the mirror.

"Well nosey, there is nothing to tell. He was hungry and so was I. That's it."

"Bitch please, you talking to me. It had to be more than dinner by the way you were smiling ear to ear getting into that nice ass Maserati."

"Just because I was getting into his car don't mean that I'm walking down the aisle."

"It sure looked like it was something. I thought we were best friends, but I see we aren't."

She just wouldn't let this subject die and kept up her interrogation.

"Girl, it's not that serious. He's feeling me, but I don't see him like that. He's cool, fun, and nice to talk to. You know who I been dealing with, so I'm not used to being in good company. So if he wants to hang out from time to time, then I'm not going to object."

"Are you sure? Cause you know how you are with men, falling in lust an all."

"What's with all the questions? You like him or something?" I asked.

Aja laughed like it was impossible for her to ever like Hasa. It came to mind, but I quickly dismissed her as a possible backstabbing bitch.

"Not even . . ." she sucked her teeth.

"I'll talk to you later." I ended blocking out everything she'd just said.

Through trial and error, I perfected my craft. I didn't have time to waste on insignificant broke dudes. I set my sights higher to get the most out of the hustle.

I was hired as a one night stand before Isaiah gets married in two days. This setup wasn't going to be anything different that I haven't already been doing, so I was cool with the arrangement. I looked at my business phone where I stored his information. Little did he know, his life is about to change.

"Are you Isaiah?"

He smiled, letting me inside of the ranch-style house.

"Yes you must be Egypt."

"Yes I am."

"Please don't think that I do this often. My friends insisted on me going out on top. No pun intended."

He chattered.

"Shish, you're rambling. There is no need for you to explain anything to me."

I overlooked Isaiah's puny demeanor because his five-hundred dollar investment was going to get me much better living arrangement.

"You so right . . . sorry . . ." he said nervously.

"Listen, we're all grown, consenting adults just looking for a good time. So how about I make us some drinks and we can start our evening. Where's your kitchen?"

The massive smirk appeared on his tan face as he pointed down the winding hallway. I shook my head because it was so sad that people can be so trusting to the point that it can cause their downfall. I knew better than most. I was a total stranger, but just because the outside was pretty, he had no idea what type of person I really could be . . . just ask the eight other dudes that met Egypt.

After mixing two Rum and Cokes, I added *liquid ecstasy* into the drink and headed back to the living room.

"You are so pretty." he said taking the drink from me.

"Thank you." I responded.

Isaiah put the glass up to his mouth and drank.

"Lets go into the bedroom where we can get a little more comfortable." he suggested.

Lately, I've been feeling like I have a vendetta against every man I come across now that Brian wronged me so many times. Most of the things that he was doing behind my back I knew about, but how deep it went was another story. I bet Isaiah's fiancée knew nothing. I bet he lied to her, saying that he had to work late all the while plotting his night with me. All men are the same, now that I know that, it is me against them.

The liquid was doing its thing quicker than I expected. I never used this method to get what I wanted before, but it was going to bring me the same outcome. I sat on the green striped chair watching him stumble around the barely used bedroom. His words were slurred, and he was sweating puddles.

"Come here."

He patted the empty space on the king-sized, canopy bed. I moved closer to him as the anticipation of what he thought he was going to get aroused him. I rubbed his slender body down with coconut oil.

"I love you Egypt." he slurred.

"Tell me that in the morning."

Isaiah passed out without another word. I shook him a couple of times to make sure he was finished. I took out my phone catching him in different compromising situations. He couldn't deny what was now clear. When I was done, I got out of the bed and went into his wallet and around the room, taking what I was entitled to. He thought that he could insult me with five-hundred dollars and think that I would just settle. I did that for so long, and I was done with that life. Without looking back, I got into my car and headed to the expressway.

"Mia, there is somebody at the door," Hasa said with a hint of worry in his voice. "Did you hear me?"

He shook me hard. I wasn't worried or hiding anything, so whoever was at my door was going to get exactly what they were looking for tonight.

"Go and get it." I said turning over when he eased out of the bed and left the room.

He couldn't have been gone a full minute before he burst back through the bedroom door frantically. I never lifted my head from the firm pillow until he spoke.

"You need to come out here now!" he yelled.

I jumped out of the bed without knowing what was going on. Aja sat shivering on the couch half naked, wearing a short black dress and one spiked heel. The silver makeup that she had on from the club was smudged. Aja had obviously been crying because black streaks of mascara stained her petrified face. She parted her dry lip but nothing came out.

"Speak! What happened to you? Did you get rapped? Robbed? What happened!" I yelled.

Hasa gave her a blanket and stood directly in front of her face, waiting for the answers to my questions.

"Girl, what happened!" he yelled getting agitated by her silence.

"I'm sad," she cried. "I'm tired of going home alone."

This girl sent my blood over the boiling point for no good reason. Aja was drunk, staggering over her words and carrying on like somebody had brutally attacked her.

"Girl please with the dramatics. You come up here like something really went down! You need to get your mind right!" I said angry that she interfered with my evening with bullshit.

"I'm sorry can I stay here with you tonight?" she asked sniffing.

I looked at Hasa as he hunched his shoulders. For the most part, he was easy going and didn't have an opinion on minor issues. I always had the last say. My gut was telling me to call her drunk ass a cab, my mind was telling me to trust no one, and my heart was telling me that I couldn't turn away a friend. I felt this way because when tempted, even friends can turn into enemies over curiosity.

"Take the kids room." I said against my better judgment.

29

"Wassup?" I asked walking into my apartment and seeing what my decision had caused.

Aja and Hasa were sitting uncomfortably on the couch silent. But their nonverbal communication said more than I wanted to hear. My burning eyes stayed on them until I got the partial truth, because they wasn't stupid enough to tell me the truth. My gut feeling was killing me internally making it hard for me to determine if I was going to beat her ass or let her pass. I waited for someone to say something.

"Nothing." they said in unison.

She crossed her legs showing her bare thigh. This bitch had the audacity to sit under my man half naked. He tried to keep one eye on me while the other focused on her finer assets. I snapped my finger in his face.

"I'm over here, not there!"

The tables were turning in the wrong direction, and it was ruining everything I'd work hard for. Something went down in here, but I wasn't expecting them to be honest with me. I knew that I shouldn't have allowed her to stay under the same roof as my man. I did, and now I regretted it.

"I'm not going to play this game with y'all. What did I walk in on?" I asked again.

"Mia, stop being paranoid." she said, walking away without speaking a hint of truth.

I was alone with Hasa. I knew him long enough to know that he was nervous about something. The temperature in my living room was seventy-two degrees and sweat drenched his Nike t-shirt. He wouldn't look at me.

"I need to get to the club and open up." was all that came out of his lying mouth.

"That's all you're gonna' say to me?" I asked.

"What more do you need me to say? Babe, you already got your mind convinced that something went on between me and your best friend. So my telling you nothing happened again would be meaningless."

Hasa moved around me leaving me to draw my own conclusion as to what I had happened before I walked in.

If I needed to dismiss some fake-ass people out of my life for the sake of my business and sanity that's what I was going to do. Although that shit that happened earlier was still eating me up inside, I had to put that aside for now.

Stripping has its stigma attached to it, but it has brought me nothing but good. For the past month, I've been enjoying the tax free easy money and the perks that came along with the job. My bank account had five stacks in it and my kids were eating more than once a day. My cherry on the top was that Brian had been MIA for weeks and there is no love loss about his decision to abandon us again.

My kids were eating steak, eggs and cheese at Isaiah's expense. I was so happy to see them because they had been at my dad's house since I started dancing. My dad thinks that I'm working at the hospital at night cleaning, but its obvious that he knows nothing about me. Even though I haven't been here physically for my babies, they had every game for their Xbox, the latest clothes, toys and food. In the fall when they go back to school, they are going to a private school. My kids wasn't wanting for nothing. They are happy with their *good life*, but it still isn't enough, they deserve more. They needed a house with a backyard and I am going to make it happen.

I sat on the counter smiling at my kids as I waited for the call. I expected to hear from Isaiah real soon because I'm sure he got the message that I sent to him a few minutes ago.

"I'm getting married tomorrow. Don't do this to me." he whispered in the phone.

"What does that mean to me? You wasn't thinking about her when you were *with* me . . . now were you?"

"That's the thing, I don't remember anything after you fixing us drinks."

"You don't remember? I'm so hurt, because I remembered everything," I said holding my chest as if he was watching my every dramatic move. "You don't have to worry about remembering because now you have the pictures for proof," I informed him. "Do you want me to send the video?"

"What do you want? I mean, you must want something other than what you stole from my wallet."

"You're a real estate agent, I need a house and you're going to give me the down payment and find me one. Please don't insult me by getting me some dump in the hood either."

He was silent when I heard a female's voice in the background asking him who he was on the phone with.

"Is that your pretty, little, unsuspecting soon-to-be wife? I wonder what she would say knowing she's about to marry a cheater?"

I didn't expect him to answer that rhetorical question but he did.

"I'm not."

"Denial is a pathetic display for a man . . . its not attractive so stop! Be a man and admit your bullshit!" I lashed out on him forgetting for a moment that he wasn't Brian.

I was now pacing the floor. He knew exactly what the purpose of this call was about two minutes ago, but he still wasn't getting it. He huffed into the phone probably regretting the day he ever met me.

"I can get you three-thousand today, but I can't do anything about the house until I get back from my honeymoon." he said as if he was doing me a favor.

"Um, do you think that my kids should have to wait while you and your wife are laying on some damn beach while we're sleeping behind the liquor store living out of my car! Hell no, you must be out of your damn mind! That's not good enough! You are gonna' work it out . . . like you did last night."

"Meet me at the Lexington Plaza at five." he gave in.

I laughed to myself when I looked down at my watch, and it said 7:13. Isaiah thought that this shit was a joke, but it was real. I meant what I said, but now that he didn't take me seriously, he was going to find out the level of my seriousness when I show up at his wedding tomorrow. I sped off down the street because I was already late for my dinner date.

I looked up from my chicken parmesan. He was aggressive when it came to getting married, his money and me. I was finally coming into my own, making money, traveling, and having so much fun that I never considered his question. I wonder if this was a question he asked Aja before I walked in on them the other day. I shook the possible answer out of my head and focused on what I was really keeping him around for. Truth-be-told, I think kept him around because his father was the owner of the club, and he gave me exactly what I wanted and needed. More so, if I let him go then Aja would have the prime opportunity to take refuge in my shelter. Besides that, he was just a cork for my slow leak. And now that someone was threatening to pry it out, I had to eliminate the problem before I lose everything. Maybe I'll tell him what I know he wants to hear until I get rid of her.

"I never thought about it, Hasa." I said.

"I love you Mia, and I feel like its time for me to meet your kids so that we can take things to the next level," he added. "Normally I don't date women with kids, but I love you enough to come out of my comfort zone.

He was wanting more than I was willing to give him at that time. I needed to find a way to slow things down, especially since he was pushing to meet my kids. I was going to protect my babies no matter what, especially since I knew that he was just like every other disappointment in my life. It was bad enough that they had a father like Brian, so I definitely wasn't going to subject them to a variety of *Uncles*. I needed to let Hasa know that we weren't at that point in our friendship for a family affair.

I coughed because of the awkwardness of the moment had suffocating effects. Hasa was 6'4, and two hundred and thirty-pounds of solid sexiness. I couldn't stop looking into his dreamy-brown eyes. He waited for my response, nervously rubbing his hands over his precise Sunni. I watched silently as he tensely sat back in the booth at the *Halal* restaurant. Damn I wanted him so bad, remembering our many nights together.

"I love you too." I managed.

He smiled, but I was empty inside. I knew exactly what he needed and what he wanted to hear, and as long as he was paying, I was going to give him just what he wanted.

"I want you to stop dancing." he sprung on me.

I pushed my plate away because suddenly I lost my appetite. This was what I was dreading: the control. Foreign men were known to be controlling, and he proved the stereotype true when he opened his mouth and told me to stop dancing.

"This is not what we're gonna' do Hasa. I don't know what you are used to, but I'm not going to allow you or any other man to dictate what I do with my life.

"No woman of mine is going to disgrace me either."

Hasa is stressing me out. He want me to stop dancing . . . smhh.

I secretly sent the text to Aja under the table. I needed her to take my mind off of his issues which he was trying to force on me; even though I thought that she crossed me.

She responded.

Hasa is sweet. All he's trying to do is take care of you, something Brian never did. Just give him a chance,

You don't understand. Just because he's giving me money and stuff doesn't mean he's better for me.

When are you going to let go?

She asked.

How can you let go of something that you never had?

I answered.

If you keep playing with his heart you are going to lose a good man.

I ignored her last comment because for the first time, she wasn't understanding where I came from.

"I'm not. I'm doing me . . . taking care of my responsibilities," I told him. "You didn't have a problem with me dancing when we first me . . ." I said.

"You can do that with a nine-to-five. And when we first met, you was just another dancer. Now that I got to know you, things are different."

"Please. With three kids? No nut-ass, minimum-wage job is going to get me what I deserve." I said ignoring his last comment.

I wasn't going to apologize or change the fact that I was loving the new me. This is the first time I can remember not wearing or accepting any second-hand items from anybody. So the subject of changing my occupation was not up for debate. If he thought that I was going to quit the hustle just to be with him, then he could think again. No one was going to take this from me.

"Well, I can just tell my father to fire you." he said boldly.

"And then do you think that I'm going to be with you?"

"I'm never going to let you go." he said with a creepy confirmation of his plans for me.

"I'm going to the ladies room." I said getting up from the table.

After walking out on him at the restaurant, I had no intension on continuing my dealings with him. But what he told me stuck to me like cheap-polyester material. Some people couldn't understand that everything wasn't for everybody. I can share some of that blame because instead of putting out the fire, I let it fester out of control. Damn, if I really didn't care about him the way I said that I didn't, I wouldn't be stressing over him. I couldn't fool my heart. This is exactly what I wanted to avoid.

"Hey are you busy?" I asked Kim.

I sat in my car recalling what had just happened. My cousin of all people could take me out of any bad funk that I was in. And at 2 a.m., I needed her now.

"Not for you. How are you?" she asked in a groggy voice.

I let out a deep breath. This conversation could go against me. And right now, I couldn't take her possible judgment. I wasn't going to go into full detail about where and when I met him. I needed some bias advice that will go in my favor.

"I'm okay. I just wanted to talk to you about my situation. I met this guy name Hasa and he wants to get serious, but I'm not ready for that. I'm not even over Brian and if I take him seriously, it might only be a rebound. I can't afford to make any more mistakes."

"Baby, every day we wake up, life is not going to be free of mistakes. You have to do what makes you happy. I told you that for years. If you love him, be with him. No man is perfect. So, what are you going to do?"

That's all I keep hearing, *what am I going to do?* If I had the answer I wouldn't be needing advice. I let out a deep breath.

"I don't have a clue. I'm going to call you back."

"Okay baby."

I got out in front of Aja's house after I made it home and decided to turn back around. After knocking on the door for half-an-hour, she didn't answer. I called and her phone was going straight to voicemail. When I saw her car and truck in the garage I knew that she was home, but was ignoring me. I banged on her wooden door when I heard the locks click open.

"Girl, what are you doing? You trying to avoid me?"

I laughed.

The only thing that was visible was her head peaking out at me in the muggy Spring air. Her face was unsettling and the vibe of suspicion was strong.

"What are you doing here?" she asked.

I found that a rather odd question to ask since our relationship always consisted of an open door policy.

"Um, I needed to talk." I humored her.

I stared at her because she was acting strange to say the least.

"Now is not a good time, I wish you would have called before you came all the way out here. I could have saved you a trip."

My eyes were stretched pass her into her house. It was dark inside and there was no sign of her children. My female intuition was on high alert because my *best friend* was defiantly hiding something that she didn't want me to know about.

"Oh . . ." I said.

"Aja!"

My heart sank and she closed her eyes. Hasa came into view and I knew what it was.

"I see now. You been fuckin' my man this entire time."

"Mia, its not what you think." she whispered.

Its not what I think. I laughed. She was fuckin' my man and it wasn't what I thought. What was it then?

I stared him directly in his face before I turned and left the two of them to what I just interrupted.

"Mia wait!" he said running after me.

I turned around before I got into the car.

"I'm glad that I been sleeping with your father." I said striking a devastating blow to his heart as well as his ego.

30

Last night was the worst night of my life and surprisingly it didn't involve Brian. My life was spiraling out of control even though I made some *positive* changes. I was kicking my own ass because I didn't apply the cardinal rule of *keeping my friends close, and my enemy even closer,* in my life. I wasn't trying to hear whatever Aja had to say. That's why when she called I disregarded her just like she did our friendship. Aja was dead to me and if she came in my face, I was going to make that statement true to my word.

My mind wouldn't rest as I slept because all that I could think about was what had went down and what I didn't know. I had so many questions, but at least I can pinpoint when it first started. I got out of my bed. Everything that reminded me of him and her had to go. After I tied the Hefty bag, I took it to the dumpster closing this chapter in my life.

Staying at home worrying myself sick wasn't going to accomplish anything. Just like they had been enjoying each other's company, tonight I was going to do the same. I walked into the *Blue Martini,* looking for relief and I was fine with whatever the night brought me.

I fought with the concept of taking a drink. I never had the desire to drink because of what it did to my mother and eventually our entire family. I knew that with her disease, it could have possibly been hereditary and I didn't need that on top of everything else bad in my life. But I wasn't getting any relief on my own, so I kept the liquor flowing.

"Is this seat taken?" he asked.

"Only when you sit down it will be." I responded, licking the aftermath from my lips.

I faced the short, hazelnut brown, good-looking guy with the darkest curly hair I ever seen. I chugged the third drink for the evening. Before I decided to be more aggressive after seeing that he was a little timid, the liquor courage had me feeling relaxed. I had to get him used to me because he was my rebound for the evening.

"I'm Egypt."

He looked around before he spoke as if his situation might walk-in on us at any moment.

"Egypt, its nice to meet you. Are you waiting for someone?"

"Before I answer that, do I at least get a name?"

"I'm sorry, its Cory."

Cory extended his hand and a bright smile crossed his face. In this dark place it was a chain reaction because despite how I felt when I walked into this bar, I was smiling now.

"To answer your question I'm not waiting for anyone."

His dimples never left the pit of his cheeks as he waived the bartender over to us.

"What is a pretty female like you doing here alone?"

"It's a long story. My so called best friend fucked my dude and now I'm here, well actually that wasn't a long story," I laughed. "But I guess that's life."

Cory was a total stranger to me. But after a few shots of *Bacardi Gold,* I told him all of my business. I didn't really care, because I needed to get that poison out of me in order for me to move on. Besides, I didn't care if he judged me because I was never going to see him again after tonight.

"The only way I know how to be is honest, so would you like me to give you my remedy? Because I know your pain all too well."

"I'm listening."

At this point I would accept any advise to stop this agonizing pain.

"A one night stand . . ." he blurted.

"I never had one of those before." I said as if it was an item off of a menu.

As old as I was, I really never had a one night stand. But to help me through the night, I was going to take him up on his offer. I'm glad that he suggested it because I was too much of a lady to suggest it.

"Well babe, there is a first time for everything."

"You can follow me back to my place." I said.

We got back to my place and I wasn't feeling any pain. Here was Cory, available, horny and naked in my living room and mine for a few hours, because that was all I needed to get over this hump. I rubbed my hands across his un-kept body. To me kissing was intimate, but the liquor had me stepping out of my comfort zone into a place where there were no rules.

The candles flickered bouncing silhouettes off the naked walls. I had him pinned down on the couch as he ripped the leopard shirt off my moist body. The summer's night heat glided through the open window. Excited by what he presented to me I knew that I wasn't going to have any remorse about this decision.

My skirt was secured around my waist like a tight belt. Cory's hands were everywhere and my mind was finally freed by this total stranger. It sounded like a bomb had just exploded in my living room. I opened my eyes and Hasa was standing in the room after he kicked my door in.

"What in the hell are you doing!" he yelled.

This warranted *unfaithfulness,* so he thought was justified in my mind. I wasn't sure if I was more mad about the door or him blowing my high. I jumped up from Cory's lap still in an exposed state. Everything was moving in slow motion as if this was some sort of dream. Hasa was so focused on me that he ignored Cory. As the excessive heat generated from Hasa's puffed-up body, I stood uncaring about his feelings. When I saw Cory's naked ass slide out the door like a snake in the grass, I shook my head. Men were truly only good for one thing.

"Since you wasn't talking to me I followed you to that bar. And when I saw you leave with him, I knew exactly what type of person you are! Allah only knows how long you have been cheating on me." he added shaking his head.

I didn't care what came out of his mouth, I was not forgetting or taking ownership of his guilt.

"Sort of like I felt when I came to Aja's house that night? And I realized you was fuckin' her behind my back?" I asked.

"Mia, I'm sorry for what I did. But what I did is no reason to give your body to many random man! You don't even know him and look at you: drunk and half naked. Where is he now? He ran out on you!"

"Its no worst than what you did to me. Would I have gotten your approval if it was with somebody you knew?"

"I can't believe you just said that."

He scowled at me.

"Besides, its better to have given my ass to a stranger, because I knew what to expect. I thought that I knew you and look what you did to me. Hasa you broke my heart . . ."

"I know I was wrong and there is no excuse good enough to justify me sleeping with Aja." he finally admitted and now I wanted to know more.

"When did all of this happen?" I asked.

He took it upon himself to sit down. I watched him drop his head in shame as he was about to explain in detail when they made the conscience decision to stab me in the back.

"That night she came to the apartment drunk. Well the next day when you went to the grocery store she walked in on me in the shower. I told her that we shouldn't do this, but she took off her clothes and got into the shower with me and it happened,"

"How many times?" I asked resting weakly against the wall.

"Mia, don't do this . . ."

"Why? What could possibly go wrong that hasn't already? So answering my questions won't make any difference, its over anyway."

"Three times. The first time was an accident, but . . ."

The brutal honesty stunned me. My body lost complete balance as I slid down the wall. Here she was, karma, with her nonsense again. How do you accidentally take your clothes off and have sex with you're friends' man? This was all bullshit.

"I hope you enjoyed your time with me because it's over." I repeated.

He looked at me as if I was joking. I grabbed my car keys and bag walking towards the door.

"I want to stay with you tonight."

"No, that's not necessary because I'm going to get my kids because they will never hurt me."

Brian's fist landed against my face and head. The last couple of night's drama left me groggy and incoherent. I wasn't expecting him since it'd been weeks since he made his last contact. Falling off the sofa bed I landed on the floor. He stood over me kicking me and throwing rapid punches which left me staggered. Brian never displayed anger like this before even when he was at his breaking point. What he couldn't begin to comprehend is that what goes around comes around.

"You stupid whore!"

I couldn't make out what he said because the last blow to the left side of my head left a deafen ringing in my ear. My babies watched in fear as their screaming and crying forced the end of my attack. I sobbed trying to catch my breath so that I could get some answers.

"What did I do?"

Brian's horns were visible. He reached in his pocket and handed me his phone.

"Yo nephew, I've been in love with Mia ever since you brought her to meet me. You treat her and your kids like shit and she deserves better. That's why we been seein' each other while you been doin' you. Make no mistake about what I'm saying to you, she leaving your sorry ass for me. Blood is thicker than water, but not in this case."

I wasn't so sure about Omar now that he went behind my back after four years and put our affair all out there. I don't feel bad about my choice, but he didn't give me the satisfaction of confronting Brian with this heartbreaking information. I rubbed my face because it was killing me. How could Brian feel any type of way for me doing what he does to me all the time? There was not a logical response that I could give him to make him feel any better, because it was the truth. This was just a little taste of how he made me feel every since I met him. There was more pain coming for Brian, I just hope he could handle it, when it arrived at his front door.

"Explain!" he spewed in anger.

I shook my head.

"My Uncle? Mia?"

"Do you expect me to apologize? I mean, really . . . do you think that I feel sorry for you or what I've done?" I asked still holding my face waiting for his response.

His eyes widened.

"Let me ask you this . . ."

I stood up holding my ribs, looking him directly in his dark eyes showing no fear. This life was catching up with him, aging him rapidly. Now I was wondering what I ever saw in an evil man like this. Now that his looks were fading he had nothing. I was glad that Kera unburdened me, now that I saw what life had to offer me.

"Did you feel bad for me when you started fuckin' Kera and got her pregnant. Or when you let our kids go hungry, or you believing that bitch and getting the water and electric cut off? That's just within the past two months! How the fuck do you think I felt for so long? Huh! Just like you tell me all the time, deal with it!"

He had nothing to say and I accomplished what I set out to do.

I went into the bathroom locking the door behind me just in case he had the courage to come back for more. I wish that I had that nerve much sooner because it felt damn good to see him finally shatter after so long. What was once up finally came down.

"Kim." I whispered through the phone.

I was in the mirror examining the bruises that I received compliments of Brian. I stuffed cotton in my ear to stop the ringing that he caused because of his insecurities that he had for a woman that he had but didn't want. I came out of my zone when she spoke.

"What's wrong?" she sounded concerned.

"I'm going to take you up on your offer." I said ready to make moves beyond my comfort zone.

"Oh . . ." her voice relaxed. "For a moment I thought . . . ."

She breathed deeply.

"No, I'm good."

"I'm happy you're coming, now I get to see you and my god kids."

"No, not this time. It's about me and having a good time. I just have that feeling that I'm gonna' find it in Philly."

"There is no doubt about that. I'm going into court, I'll call you when I get done."

"Okay."

I left the bathroom. Brian didn't leave anything on me that a little foundation couldn't cover. I walked pass him saying nothing. He opened his mouth when I closed the door leaving him to be a father for a few hours.

Hurt can make people do things that they may regret. There was no emotional ties to Isaiah, so he is going to be the only one that is going to have regrets after this.

Greater A.M.E was full of people watching this couple commit to spending the rest of their lives together. I looked around bringing up old dreams of what will never happen between me and Brian. I fought back the tears in order to get through this moment.

"Does anyone see why these two shouldn't be married, speak now or forever hold you peace . . ."

My mind and any sense of right and wrong left me a long time ago. The deep gasps and soft whispers floated mid air. I stepped out into the aisle letting the accusations and assumptions circulate around me. I spoke.

"I object!"

All eyes were on me wondering what rock I crawled from under to do such a thing like this and of all days. Why in the hell would I choose any old normal day to ruin lives? This was a special occasion that they would remember forever.

For the moment no one said anything because the severity of the situation wasn't sinking in. If Isaiah wasn't clear about my demands before, he got how serious I was now.

"Babe, you can't do this to me . . . you can't leave me . . . I love you!" I yelled releasing all my pain on this very moment.

I painted a believable picture that he wasn't even sure of. Isaiah shook his head so hard that I thought it was going to fall off his shoulders. His fiancée snatched her hands away from him with a blank look on her sad face. While I walked their red satin runner, I realized that he must have dropped at least fifty-thousand on the wedding alone. White doves sat on both sides of the platform in gold cages. Two sets of spiral staircases held the wedding party elegantly. It was all about image to everyone and it annoyed the hell out of me.

"You stupid bitch . . ." he mumbled.

I winked at him because I finally got his attention.

"No . . ." she whispered.

"Isaiah don't do this to me! I love you and I want to be with you,"

He turned towards me.

"You get your crazy ass outta' here!"

"Don't worry about it because I'm leaving and I never want to see you ever again." she said to her fiancé.

We watched as she took her platinum ring off and dropped it at his feet. I felt for her, but this was about him not making good on his promise. She lifted her white silk gown as she stepped off her petal stool.

"Bree wait!" he yelled.

He stopped inches from away from my face. With a hateful scowl on his face he spoke.

"You're gonna' regret the day you ruined my life. The same way you found me, I will find you."

He ran from the chapel trying to salvage the ruins compliments of Egypt.

31

The sixteen hour Greyhound bus ride left me sticky and worn-out. I needed this and should have done it sooner. But worrying about what Brian was doing caused me to miss out on life. It's been about four-and-a half years since I physically seen Kim, so I didn't have any idea as to who I was spending the weekend because its obvious that our life had taken two very different paths. I really didn't care because it just felt damn good to be released from my everyday drama.

Just the thought of this fast pace city life excited me. I stood on the corner of Filbert Street smiling and inhaling the smog of the city when a 2014 Aston Martin Volante pulled up in front of me. Kim left me feeling even more insecure than happy now that I was seeing how her hard work has paid off. Why was something so good about to make me cry? My embarrassment kept me away for so long but it was obviously for the best. This was suppose to be me.

The sultry heat stung my warm body as I rubbed my hand across the sexy body of the car. I opened the door and caressed the Monaco red leather seats. The new car smell consumed me as I forced myself to forget about the empty choices that caused me to miss out on all of this.

"You look so beautiful." Kim said which I didn't believe a single word of.

I knew that I looked nothing like I should have. I tried to fake it as much as I could. This multi-colored Maxi dress and eight hundred dollar sandals that I had on was nothing compared to her expensive: one piece backless olive jumper and gold snakeskin sandals. I knew that she wasn't strapped for money. I was just hoping that it wasn't an eviction notice taped to my door when I got home. Her lifestyle made me want to jump into the dumpster along with the rest of the trash.

"I missed you so much." she continued hugging on me tight.

My resentment was geared in the wrong direction. I resented my cousin for succeeding in the dreams that we had planned ever since childhood. At twenty-six she was a junior corporate attorney at the firm Montague, Kline and Baker Inc. Her car, clothes and the pictures of her home on the Mainline had the same effect on me as loosing my mother. It's obvious that I'd been cursed and for that, I was mad at God. How could he allow these things to happen to me? I wasn't perfect but I deserved at least a fraction of what she had and since I couldn't have my mom back, I was going to see to it that I got the materialistic aspect of the deal. I took a deep breath and put on a fake smile and returned the anticipated hug.

"You look great too." I said dryly.

The manner in which I gave the compliment went directly over Kim's head.

"We have a lot of catching up to do." she said.

While we drove through downtown, I completely ignored her chatty rambling. I really didn't have a lot of good news to share because there wasn't anything promising about the life that I was living. Meanwhile, I was trying to figure out my next move because this trip was temporary.

Shopping, lunch and the spa had me exhausted but relaxed. I couldn't remember the last time that I laid in a bed. The simple things that is taken for granted was a luxury to me which was depressing. I sat up in the bed when I heard the faint knock on the door.

"Come in."

I had a tendency to wear my emotions on my face. I forced a content look to mask the real truth before Kim decided to start asking questions.

"Do you need anything?"

"Fun." I said

Kim laughed.

"Then I suggest you get dressed I have the perfect place." she said leaving me alone.

After standing in her whirlpool shower savoring every moment, I didn't think twice about Georgia. That place was holding me back. And the first chance I got to move on, I was taking it. I picked through the outfits that Kim bought for me today. I loved having options, it made me feel special. I sat in the mirror finishing up my makeup when Kim walked in without knocking.

"How do I look?" I asked standing up from the gold brass vanity.

I tugged at the stone mini dress that resembled a bathing suit more than a dress.

"You look beautiful." she responded.

That statement made me even more emotional. Something as simple as a compliment meant so much to me. I haven't heard or felt like this in a long time.

"What's wrong?" she asked because she would have never understood my plight.

"I don't deserve this."

"What to be loved and treated as a human being?"

"Yes, that and this." I said pointing from my two-hundred dollar sew-in, to the fifty dollar makeup, to the one hundred-and-fifty dollar scooped front dress and the red bottom heels.

"What did he do to you?"

She shook her head refusing to let the tears ruin her makeup.

"Not love me that's for sure. I've been homeless, I live in the projects, I have no job and I'm here pretending that I'm special." I blurted truthfully.

"I'm gonna' really hurt you! As long as I'm here, you have nothing to worry about. That's the past and this is the first day of the rest of you life."

She wrapped her arms around me. The memories of my mother holding me as a child came flooding back.

"I wish I could believe that." I cried.

"You don't have to, you'll see." Kim spoke my change into existence.

If this was going to be my night and the only one that I will have to myself, I was going to make the most of it. I looked at Kim as if she forgot to mention this part of her life, because club *Entyce* was filled with women.

"Don't even go there. I know what you're thinking. It's male exotic entertainment at its finest." she laughed.

"Strippers!" I beamed excitedly.

"Shish . . ." she laughed. "You need this, besides you said that you wanted to have fun. Here you have your fun, fantasy, seduction, sexy ass men and freakiness all rolled up into one crazy night. It doesn't get any better than this."

When she sat back and crossed her legs I relaxed, just a little.

"Ladies are you ready for your next entertainer . . ."

The desperate women screamed.

"And here he is, the chocolate wonder, the king of erotic himself . . . . Phoenix . . ."

The flashing lights and steam filled the seventies inspired room. It was humid. I took my clutch and fanned my face in tune with every beat of the music. Above our heads was a disco ball that illuminated the situation. Surrounding the circular stage were horny women throwing their hard earned money on the empty stage. I thought to myself that this Phoenix had to be special in their eyes by the way they were acting. Me personally, I couldn't take a man serious that shook his ass for a living.

A heavy hand landed on my shoulder. I looked up into the face of the sexiest man that I've seen in a very long time. He swung his beefy legs across me rubbing my damp face. I was so embarrassed because all the attention in the room was on me. This experience left me feeling like I just climbed out of a wormhole into the new normal. Kim took a dollar bill and put it between my raised D's. Phoenix followed by taking his luscious lips kissing my breasts and extracting the money at the same time. I reached out to touch him, but I couldn't . . . I refused to and tightened my fist. I squeezed my thighs together as he took my hands and placed them on his dark chocolate chiseled chest.

I gave in and rubbed over him savoring every moment knowing that this was only a fantasy that was going to end at two.

If I thought that he was done with the tease, I was wrong. He had more in store for me which internally boost my ego. Phoenix took the tip of his tongue and traced my mango breeze scented chest. That alone almost sent me through the roof. I've seen all I needed to. I wasn't looking for anything long term, another completed one night stand would do me just fine.

"I want that . . ." I whispered not willing to take my eyes off of him in case this was a dream.

"Who?" Kim asked sarcastically.

I took my American gel manicured finger and pointed on stage at the man that aroused my sexual curiosity. I refused to look at her because I wasn't missing out on what was coming next. Phoenix's seduction had me on the edge of my seat when he removed the horizontal onyx leather straps throwing the vest off to the side. Two women swarmed the stage, one seasoned and out of shape and the other, a young Puerto Rican with long black hair and skin the color of buttermilk. I noticed every detail about her because she threw at least two hundred ones on him. Everywhere he moved she followed him like a love sick puppy dog. When she walked off stage switching in her *Apple Bottom* jeans, I quickly dismissed her.

"I'll be back." I said getting up from the nicked table only after he exited the stage.

The smoky cramped bathroom had me holding my breath. Stepping out into the dimly lit hallway I exhaled quickly drawing it back in when I saw Phoenix. I wasn't trying to assume anything but I was hoping that he was waiting for me.

"I thought you left." he said.

I looked over my shoulder making sure that no one walked out of the restroom behind me.

"No not yet."

"Let me introduce myself, I'm Phoenix."

I smiled.

"I know, I'm *Summer*. It's nice to meet you."

"That's a pretty name and my favorite season." he added suavely.

"That's good to know, we have something in common," I said trying to move around him nervously. "I need to get back to my sister."

I took one step forward before he grabbed my arm.

"Wait, why are you in such a hurry?"

"Um to finish watching the show."

"Trust me, you ain't missing nothing. Let's go to breakfast." he suggested.

I thought for a moment, but not too long. Life has taught me that opportunities don't have a long shelf life, so I had to make a decision.

"Let me go and tell my sister that suddenly there is a welcomed change of plans."

Kim didn't mind me ditching her as long as I was having a good time, even if she did feel some type of way. I would hit her with one of my many hard luck stories that would give me a free pass.

A diner . . . I thought when I stepped through the door. My face said it all and Phoenix read every word it was saying. I thought about my babies and an instant smile appeared.

"I hope you don't mind me bringing you here. This is the only place open this time of morning." he justified his decision.

I looked around the packed diner and believed everything that came out of his mouth. A common place like this didn't suit his quality personality. I wasn't going to concern myself with irrelevant details such as where he took me. Actually, I would have been satisfied with him taking me to McDonalds, just as long as somebody seen us together.

"I totally understand that this isn't how you do things. But to me it doesn't matter as long as I'm in good company."

"Damn, this is different."

"What is?" I asked.

"A female that isn't worried about lining her pockets. Or about what she can get out of the deal. In Philly, I'm not used to that. I guess it's true, there are still a few good ones left."

"And I believe that there are a few good men left as well."

But I haven't found one yet, I thought.

Phoenix reached across the table and held my hand and I drew back. Brian crept into my head bringing back some well hidden insecurities. Just because I was here with him didn't mean very much. Because my life proved that things can go wrong in a blink of an eye. And then there is a possibility that at any time Phoenix could flip the script on me. It was a hard thing to do, but I had to limit my expectations no matter how good he was treating me. I subtly shifted in my seat. His eyes never left my body which made me a little uncomfortable. I couldn't resist him, so I turned around allowing him to hold my hand. It was starting.

"Summer, tell me something . . ."

I lowered the menu. At this point, I never expected to meet anyone let alone create a new identity. I was doing good flowing with mine, but I had that feeling that he might throw me a curve by asking me something that I couldn't answer.

"What's that?" my curiosity peeked.

"Where have you been all my life? I mean, I want to know all about you; where are you from? Where have you been? Where are you going and can I come along?" he asked smoothly like a shot of Cognac Gold.

This was getting too intense for me. All of this was too good to be true. I laughed because he was surly putting his twist on things. And I loved every minute of it. But how could I forget the game that he was in. He hadn't known me long before he spun me in his web. In the process I had a temporary laps in judgment. I laughed because he almost got me. Night after night I capped dudes up, sold the fantasy just to increase my bank. If Phoenix thought that he was going to cap me up to get what I got, he had another thing coming.

Unbelieving of my new situation I sat back and shook my head. I was trying to shake the mixed feelings that I had. Before I spoke I had to be so careful not to reveal so much, because in the end it could be my downfall. I didn't like my life, so I wasn't going to let him have access to the only thing that I was trying to escape. He was going to get the story of how I desired my life to be.

"I need to know everything about the people I let in my life," he continued. "I have a lot to lose."

"I understand and agree."

If only he knew.

Phoenix laughed showing a set of pure white teeth with braces.

"You don't have to be scared to let me in." he replied.

I folded my hands on the menu and looked at him deeply. His black and white plaid shirt hugged his thick tatted arms and chest. The image of him in his fitted jeans made me horny, now I wish that I wore panties.

"What's that scent you're wearing?" I asked.

That question was one of the first ones I asked Brian. I didn't want the following events to end up like they had with Brain so I held my tongue.

"Oh you like it, its called *Blue Paradise*," he said. "But don't avoid my questions."

"You were really serious?"

I contemplated whether or not this trouble was worth getting into before I revealed my artificial me.

"Yes, but I don't mind going first."

I smiled allowing him to have center stage in my world.

"Lets see, I work at *S. F. Mills* school for boys. I'm a counselor. I'm single, born and raised in Philly, thirty-one, and I have a degree in social services, no kids and don't want any."

His requirements disqualified me as his possible mate. Mia had three kids and there was no way I could hide them either. I had the worst luck in the world.

"With all of that you have going for you, why are you a stripper?"

"I am not a stripper. I'm a *Male Exotic Entertainer.* There are a lot of women that deserve the attention that they are not getting at home. So I do it for the allure, the thrill and the fantasy," he said rubbing my cheek with the back of his hand. "I love to please women, especially my woman. Seeing the smiles on their faces when I deliver is priceless. But it's crazy how I got started. My friend Dominique dared me to do it and here I am seven years later."

"Do you think you'll ever stop?" I asked.

"If I have the right persuasion."

"Well, I'm twenty-six, my given name is Summer Jordan, single, no kids, I'm a year away from my degree in criminal justice. I'm from Florida and I'm vacationing here with my sister for the forth of July, I leave tomorrow."

I am officially a fraud and I knew he saw right through me. Everything from this moment on in our relationship is going to be built on a lie. What I told him is the life that I dreamed of. But just image if he knew Mia Latham, the person that I was trying to hide in order to make him mine.

"That's sad."

"What's sad?" I asked.

"The fact that I only have you for a short time."

My heart melted.

"I know exactly how you feel."

"Listen, I'm not really hungry. I really wanna' make every moment count so . . . lets get out of here." he told me and I was okay with that.

I stood up before he said another word.

Phoenix pulled his onyx BMW into a spot over looking boathouse row. The lights and stars made him seem angelic. I considered our chance meeting god-sent. He opened the sunroof and turned up *Can you handle it.*

"I don't believe in being indirect. I see what I want and I go for it." he told me.

Phoenix left me speechless when he got out of the car to come around to the passenger side. He took my hand and I got out. The breezy winds blew in from the river giving me the chills. Or it could have been Phoenix's gentle touch when he sat me on top of the hood of the car. Previously I based my happiness on materialistic things. But now I knew the real definition of happiness; a man's attention. It was having nothing standing in my way that had me glowing. It wasn't Brian, the kids, or Kera and I loved this uninhibited freedom.

"What are you doing?" I asked.

"Shish, I'm hungry now." he said gripping my thighs.

My moans echoed off the cool waters of Philadelphia. My quivering legs hung over his broad shoulders. The sweat and passion cause me to slid off the hood but his grip tightened allowing me to stay where I was. With one hand positioned on the car and one foot on the bumper he forced his way into my life and I welcomed the instant gratification.

32

Kim was the first thing I saw when I opened my eyes. She was so close that our noses were touching. Immediately the worst was running through my mind. Frantically I sat up in the bed ready to face what I didn't know. She smiled at me shaking her head at the same time. Then placed her hands on my shoulders to keep me in my place.

"What's wrong? Did something happen?"

"Relax, he's here." Kim whispered.

I was confused. It was too early for the guessing games. So after drawing a few blanks I hunched my shoulders.

"Phoenix is downstairs for you." she said more excited than I was.

My nerves was getting the best of me. I smiled remembering everything that happened last night. And him being here confirmed that everything that went down early this morning wasn't all in my imagination.

"Are you serious?" I asked.

Kim stood straight up and put her hands impatiently on her hips.

"Get your ass up, brush your teeth, wash your face put on this robe and take your ass downstairs."

I slid out of the bed and went into the bathroom. Instead of her going to finish her depositions she went into the closet and laid out a Champaign silk robe for me to put on.

"Maybe you should get rid of him . . ." I said reluctant to go downstairs.

"Honey, this is your time to have fun. Stop questioning everything and let it flow," she continued. "I'm not telling him nothing. You tell him yourself . . . if that's your choice.

I never got into details with her about what happened last night. Kim sensed my hesitation which she put an immediate stop to before I even had a chance to ruin the possibility. Just for a moment I had to block her out of my mind. I didn't know why he was here, but I was going to find out soon.

Phoenix was in the living room looking at the pictures on the tea table. I adjusted my robe to make me look a little more appealing.

"Hey was sup?" I said reaching the bottom of the staircase.

I was caught off guard when he grabbed me around my waist. When he stuck his tongue in my mouth I melted in his arms. What's done in the dark always come to the light. We did a lot of things last night that I'm actually glad happened. He was different than what I was used to and expected him to be. And he was changing the game and my opinion of men. I had an infatuation for him already, leaving me vulnerable to anything that he would possibly bring my way.

"Well, this is a pleasant surprise."

"Last night seemed like forever without you. I wish that you took me up on my offer to come back to my place. But since you didn't, I needed to see you ASAP." he said honestly.

"That's the sweetest thing anyone has ever said to me."

"Because it's the truth. What are you doing today?" he asked.

Shit, if I had something else to do, it was voided when he walked back into my life for the second time.

"Spending it with you hopefully."

"That's exactly the answer that I was hoping to hear. My family is having a barbeque/pool party for the forth, would you like to come?"

"Yes," I said without hesitation.

As long as I've been playing mistress to Brian, he has never attempted to take me home to his family, except for his uncle and that decision was solely for the purpose of bragging rights.

Right now I was in a good place with a good man and I wasn't going to let nothing or no one take that away from me.

"Babe, I'll pick you up at four."

He kissed me again and left the house.

I got depressed instantly. I was suppose to go back to my real life tomorrow, but I didn't want to leave my cushy life here. There was nothing for me in Sugar Hill but drama and hopelessness. Life isn't fair by playing this cruel game with my heart.

"What's wrong boo?"

Kim said sitting on the bed watching me get ready for my date.

"I haven't been this happy in a longtime. It feels like this is where I am meant to be."

"Mia, I told you, whenever you're ready to make that move, I'll help you and the kids start over." she said trying to fulfill her good deed.

"That's the thing I don't want that life anymore."

She looked at me trying to figure out what I was actually trying to say. When it wasn't making any sense to her, she flagged me.

"Gurl, you talking crazy . . . what are you going to do with your kids?" she asked putting on her inner hood chick.

"I don't know, but I think its time for Brian to figure that out. Maybe he'll see how it feels to be tied down. Then maybe he'll appreciate me and all that I did, without his help. In the meantime, I'm doing me as much as I can before I'm forced back into that other life. Honestly, I really don't give a damn anymore."

"Mia, you really don't mean that. You need to slow down. You met this stripper, he showed you a good time. I understand all of that, but that don't mean he's for you. And it damn sure ain't a sign to tell you drop everything for him. This is what they do Mia! You need to come back to reality and take things for what they are, a good time, not a lifelong commitment."

"That's your opinion, and its obvious that you don't know me like you think you do."

Kim pissed me off with her judgmental poison that she put on me at the worst time. Its fine when she's on top, but when

I finally find happiness, she shoots it down. Kim knew nothing about my situation and I don't know why I expected her to relate to me at all. As of today, I didn't need her or anyone else except for Phoenix. Without him saying so, I knew he felt the same exact way about me. My heart says so.

I left Kim's house without saying another word to her. Her thoughts on the subject filled my head threatening to ruin my afternoon. Phoenix held onto my hand willing to let everyone know that I was with him. I can get used to this life.

He took me around the large single home in Media introducing me to his successful family. This was another situation that I had to fake my way through. I kept silent.

"Summer, what do you do for a living? Do you have any kids or husband, girlfriend?" his mother Jacqueline asked offending me.

She could tell by the look on my face that I didn't appreciated her slick comment that she threw in her interrogation, so she tried to clean it up.

"I'm sorry, this is 2013 you can never be too sure."

Damn this was pathetic. Truth . . . here was that dirty word again. I was sick of it because it had no place in my life right now. I needed to wait until I secured my husband before I started divulging any type of truth. That's why she wasn't ready for my raw truth. A mother of three, hustler, stripper, husband stealer . . . that was my life. I cleared my throat and laughed nervously.

"I understand. No, I don't have any kids, girlfriends and hopefully your son can fill that husband position in the future. As far as my occupation is concerned, I am an entrepreneur . . ." I said trying to squirm out of this tight position.

I thought that was going to satisfy her curiosity, but this woman felt that she needed to pry even more.

"Really, what is it that you sell?"

I shook my head trying to keep from laughing in her elegant, cinnamon brown face.

"Actually, I'm a caterer." saying the first thing that came to mind, even though there was some truth to what I had just revealed.

"That's great, I am throwing Shaun's father a sixtieth birthday party in October. If you can fit us into your schedule I would love to hire you."

I smiled.

"Thank you." I said keeping it brief as possible.

Phoenix came and grabbed hold of my wet hand relieving my anxiety. I was glad that this conversation ended on a good note when it did. His mother was married to the chief of police, so I needed to keep my distance before she tried to start an investigation of her own. I needed to play her real close.

"Everybody loves you Summer." Phoenix whispered into my ear.

If only they knew who they were actually loving.

33

This was the day I was dreading every since I met him. It was time for me to go back home. I laid in his California king sized bed with a few unforced tears soaking my pillow. I couldn't believe that I was feeling this way about a man I hardly even knew, but has shown me more in a weekend than Brian showed me in years. I just hope these feelings don't dissipate as quickly as they came to me.

"Babe, please don't cry." he said wiping my tears.

"I know, I just been having so much fun with you."

"How about I come and visit you next weekend." he suggested.

Fear of him finding out who I really was and not who I pretended to be scared me. I would surely lose him if he found out I lived in the projects with three kids by a married minister, compared to his success. I had no real means of an income and no college degree, nor was I close to achieving one. Now that I played with that fact of being honest, I couldn't because there was nothing exotic about that life. So why would I expect him to dismiss that to carry my second-hand baggage?

"I don't want you to travel so far." I said.

"It doesn't matter as long as we're together."

I let out the hardest breath.

"I have to get ready to go now." I said reluctantly.

"I can take you to the airport." Phoenix said rubbing my shoulders striking up my desire for a goodbye quickie.

"That's okay. Since I haven't spend that much time with Kim, I promised her that she could take me. Besides, I don't want to make this harder than it has to be."

"I have to respect that." he said sadly.

Phoenix reached inside a drawer and took out a black bag.

"I got this for you."

I threw the gold-and-white frosted tissue paper aside and opened the box.

"If we never cross paths again, I'll remember you for eternity." he told me putting the white gold Eternity necklace on my neck.

I haven't been in Georgia for an hour before the bullshit had greeted me at my front door. Although the scales had tipped downward in some aspects of my getting to know Phoenix, even for me I should have known meeting him was too go to be true. I was waiting for my dream to end, but I didn't know that it would be this soon. The moment that I let my guard down and got comfortable somebody attacked full force. Some dead person kicked my door in stealing everything they could get their hands on.

I stood in the middle of the room looking at nothing that surrounded me. I still couldn't believe it. So I walked into every room shaking my head in disbelief. Everything that I worked so hard for was gone in a matter of seventy-two hours. No matter how much I rationalized what had just altered my life, I couldn't conceive having nothing all over again. This was my indication telling me to cut my losses and move on from this misery. I had to get out this place that has brought me continuous sadness.

Being back at the club is the last thing that I wanted to do, but I needed to make some quick money to replace some things before my kids were due back home. I sat on the stool in the dressing room looking over the police report when my phone rang again. My dad was over the fact that I keep dumping the kids on him. I wasn't trying to hear anything that he had to say or deal with those kids now, because if they weren't born, I wouldn't be stuck where I am. I needed figure this out without the distraction.

"Mia can we talk?"

I shoved the police report into my bag. A combination of me having to leave Phoenix and me being robbed put me in a real bad mood. I didn't want to be bothered and now that Aja was in my space adding to my existing irritation.

"I'm listening." I said with a major attitude.

"I didn't mean for things to turn out this way between the two of us." she said.

I hunched my shoulders.

"So you saying you don't regret sleeping with my dude?"

Aja hunched her shoulders uncaringly about the situation.

"Not really, because you said you wasn't feeling him." she followed-up arrogantly.

"So the hell what! That didn't mean that you had to go and spread your legs for him. I can't trust shit that you say or do! And out of all places in my house!"

"He was fair game, haven't I taught you anything? When it comes to me and doing what makes me happy, that wins hands down over anybody including you and your feelings."

Her words cut like a rusty knife straight to my already fragile heart. There was nothing that I could say to her or want to say. Because there was something that I was holding onto that no one could take away from me. So if she felt like she needed Hasa, she could have him.

"Don't walk away from me Mia! I'm not done talking to you!" she yelled.

"Well, I'm done with you bitch!"

34

I just didn't feel like being bothered. This time alone was going to allow me to sort through my screwed up life with a fine-tooth-comb.

Let me in, the message said. I got off of the floor and looked out of my front window. There were no curtains to move because they were stolen as well. Hasa was standing downstairs with some damn balloons at four in the damn morning like an escaped mental patient. This wasn't a damn carnival and he sure as hell wasn't going to take me for a ride either. I sucked my teeth but let him inside for unspoken reasons.

He landed at the top of the stairs. I had no intensions on letting him inside because I was over this life of multiple men and just as much drama that came along with them. The things that he did to me was unnecessary. Although I was hesitant to take things to the next level he didn't have to fuck me over, literally. I'm glad that I followed my gut feeling because to me there wasn't anything worst to me than being stuck in a loveless relationship again.

"Aren't you going to let me in?"

"I hadn't planned to." I responded.

"I'm sorry if you feel that way." he said handing me the bunch of pink balloons.

"Don't think you can come here with this meaningless shit and think that I'm going to forget about you screwin' my ex-best foe!"

"Actually I came here to ask you to marry me."

I laughed in his face despite the fact that my body was over-heating with anger. You would have thought that I learned my lesson from dealing with Brian, but obviously not because I was in the same place again.

"Take your damn balloons and go ask Aja to marry you! She was good enough to cheat with, so she should be good enough to marry!" I yelled shoving him out of my life.

"Once I leave here I won't be back." he threatened.

"Is that a promise?" I asked making sure he stood by his word.

Without saying another word he took his balloons and his lies and left my life. Hopefully for good.

The phone woke me up just when I finally drifted off to sleep. Without looking to see who it was I answered.

"Hello . . ." I said in a semi-conscience state.

"I need you to listen . . ."

When I heard her voice I propped up on my elbow never opening my eyes because this was going to be a short conversation.

"Before you hear it from anybody else, I'm getting married . . ." she informed me.

"So what does that mean to me?"

"Because its to Hasa. We going to do something small tomorrow at City Hall."

By the time that she told me that she was marrying the man that I was seeing I was already up on my feet digging my heels into the floor. This was the last thing that I needed on top of everything else. I especially didn't want Hasa now that he was used goods. But my blessing for them wasn't to get married. Now that it was actually happening, there wasn't a damn thing that I could do about that.

I had an extremely long day. After replacing mostly everything that was taken from me all I wanted to do was stay in tonight, sleep and be left alone. So much for that thought.

"Bitch have you lost your mind!"

"No, that's why we want you to come and be our witness."

"This shit ain't happening. After all you seen me go through you gonna' do this to me! I thought you knew me better than anyone I know. You knew damn good and well that I had feelings for him Aja!"

"What do you want me to say, I'm sorry? Well I'm sorry if that's what you need to hear. But that isn't going to stop us from getting married. On some real talk, you should sleep easy knowing that I'm not marrying him for love. His visa is about expire and he needed my help and the sex isn't bad either," she said gloating. "I couldn't turn my back on him especially for ten thousand dollar and all the sex I want," she said proudly. "We only going to live with each other temporarily until after the interview."

My head was pounding. This confirmed her jealousy from the exact moment me and Hasa started dealing with each other. But now that I replay everything over in my head, I invited her into my bedroom. I shared my escapades with her, so she had to see if the tales were true. This is why they were getting married tomorrow.

"You have his heart. You're all he talks about Mia and I'm okay with that."

After hanging up on her I analyzed every contradiction that came out of her mouth. Aja had been plotting my downfall from day one. As far as Hasa is concerned, if he was easily tempted by a shedevil, he deserved everything that she was bound to give him. Knowing that karma was going to set the record straight took away some the hurt. I was so glad that I was going to see Phoenix tomorrow.

I procrastinated this moment ever since I found out what they had been doing behind my back. It really felt like it was over. My heart wasn't in this performance, so I just associated this feeling as the end of this chapter in my life. It was bitter sweet, but I wanted to detoxify in order for me to have a clean start with Phoenix. I emptied the rest of my things into my bag. The only thing that was on my mind was getting out of here before I did something to Aja or Hasa that I necessarily might not regret.

I held my final check in my limp hand and hugged Akee tightly.

"You sure you don't want to reconsider?"

"I'm very sure." I said to Akee before leaving this life forever.

The fresh rain beat down on me as I put the key into the lock.

"Bitch you move or scream I'm gonna' blow your head off." the voice suggested in a low raspy tone.

Paralyzed with my phobia of having a gun up to my head I drew a blank. Of all times, the unwanted was wanted, but no one was around but the person that wanted to take my life from me just because.

"Please, I have kids." I begged.

"You should have thought about that before . . ." he chose not to continue his statement.

This man refused to let me look at him and I'm not sure if I wanted to either. I felt him shaking as much as I was and I was the victim. This was a lonely dark place to be in. I thought that what I'd been through with Brian was horrible. But it was nothing compared to knowing that this was my end. I never gave any thought to how I was going to die, but I never imagined that dying like this was my ultimate fate.

The stench of trash and hopelessness consumed me. For a Friday night it was too quiet except for his hard breathing and my pounding heart. He snatched the bags from my tight grip. He had everything that he came for, but he was still here with an apparent score to settle. When he allowed the handle of the .45 to connect with me repeatedly, I couldn't help but to wonder, who sent him and who would look after my babies when I die. Blow after blow I moaned in agony until my voice was silenced.

My dream was transposed that I had years ago. Instead of Traci and Brian being in the dream it was de ja vu. Time seemed to have stopped when I fell to the wet ground feeling the swelling of my face intensify. There was no way in hell that he was going to let me get out of this parking lot alive. He didn't need to say so, I just knew it. Through the tears there was a sparkle that caught my attention. If I made a sudden stupid move I would be dead, so I needed to make this count. My eyes widened when he took off the oversized hood revealing his face, I laughed.

"Isaiah . . ."

He wiped his wet forehead with the back of his hand the held the gut.

My eye felt like I was in a boxing match, but there was no mistaking him for someone else.

"You fucked with the wrong one. In less than twenty-four hours you had everything taken from me. Now I'm going to show you what I felt like when you ruined my life." he said revealing his vendetta.

"She don't even want to marry me!" he sniffed.

He cocked the gun. Everything went black.

I couldn't stop shaking even in the safety of my own home. There was blood on my clothes and my trembling hands. If I took his life in that lot, he brought death upon himself.

The hot water ran off my battered body as I watched his blood run down the drain. These were harsh warnings that was coming more frequently. This was a fight for my life. And the tight space between the rock and a hard place didn't help matters either. I had to make a decision that no one was going to be happy with, because it wasn't going to benefit them.

My intensions were to sleep when I got to Virginia cuddled in Phoenix's arms, inhaling his cologne. I was already there mentally. I stayed up all night because my mind would not stop racing and it was taking its toll on me. I thought that at any moment the police would be knocking on my door to arrest me for murder. Now that the dust had settled, I put everything in order. No matter what I did to remember the truth, the story kept changing. There was a broken *Corona* bottle on the ground. Once I reached it I held onto it ready to fight for my life. Every death threat that Isaiah threw my way made me unsympathetic and cold. When it was the right time I lunged at him with full force.

The image of him laying in his own blood as I drove away flashed periodically through my head. I needed to forget, so I forced myself to think logically. This happened behind a hood strip club in the worst neighborhood in town. Just like every other crime in that area, it was going to be swept under the rug and labeled drug related because I would only know the real truth.

Sheraton Suites is where I planned on spending the next two days. Before Phoenix was due to arrive I moved around the room setting the mood and making sure everything was perfect because that's what he deserved. I lit some mango candles, threw some white rose petals onto the bed and slipped into a lace shaper. I was ready for my man. The door clicked and Phoenix brought an immediate smile to my flushed face. I knew where I made my mistakes at with Brian, so I was going to be everything to Phoenix and more.

I got up from the bed taking the bag from his hand. His eyes were attached to my body when he grabbed me.

"Babe what happened to your face?" he said with genuine concern.

Obviously the transparent makeup didn't do shit to cover my bruises. He saw right through it. I was going to downplay my physical imperfections.

"Its not bad as it seems. I got into a car accident on Thursday . . ."

"How come you didn't call me? Or mention it when we talked? I would have came to take care of you . . . we could have postponed this." he had the audacity to suggest.

"I know that's why I didn't mention it." I said sadly.

"If we are going to build a life together, you have to let me in Summer."

"In due time."

I dropped the bag at our feet. His lips got reacquainted with my body and I remembered our steamy memories of Philly. I wasn't giving this up because this time was just as good as the first.

I laid in the bed next to my future, planning out my life with him. The only thing is that I needed to drop subtle hints about my plans for us. I knew that I said after Brian that I wasn't going to plan a life with anybody else, but this man was different. I didn't have to worry about competing with a wife or girlfriends. This minor detail to some made him much better than what I was used to. Anything else that might come up later, I was going to turn a blind-eye to his flaws. It couldn't be worst than Brian's constant bullshit.

"Babe is everything okay? You seem distant?" he asked.

"I'm just taking in every moment of my time with you."

He smiled kissing me on my cheek. I had to be selective in what I was going to say because I didn't want to run him away. Among other things, I was going to minimize my issues.

"That may be true, but there is something else." he said.

Phoenix turned to me showing off his cut body. I said nothing because his sexiness was distracting. I rubbed on him while I tried to form my words.

"I can't trust no one." I blurted out.

Saying the first thing that came to mind, I quickly regretted it.

"Is it me?" he asked.

I shook my head so hard that the room spun.

"Absolutely not. You have been nothing but perfect."

"I'm not perfect, but I'm perfect for you." he admitted.

"I truly believe that you are Phoenix."

He took my hand and kissed the back of it.

"I was talking about my ex-best friend. She told me that she was marrying a person that I've dealt with before."

"Do you still have feelings for him?"

Without hesitation I responded.

"No, it's just that out of all the people in state, she chose him."

I lowered my head remembering the night I caught the two of them together.

"It sounds like she's just jealous of you. Why else would she dig through your leftovers? But don't let that worry you. You have me now Summer and I love you."

Again, he couldn't love what he didn't know. Phoenix loved who I was pretending to be. With my lies, I'm glad that I got this far with him, so I decided to say nothing.

35

All I had been doing every since I got back from my trip a month ago was smile. The situation that I am in is manageable now that Phoenix gave me something to hang my hopes on. Although he hasn't made this official I made up in my mind that I was done with all the guys from my past, even though Brian came back, again. And that's how I get through my days in hell.

I need to talk to you. Phoenix's message said after sending me some pictures of a house that was just built from the ground. He didn't wait for me to respond, he decided to call me. I was a little worried because this could have been some drama conjured up by his meddling mom. I held my breath.

"Hello." I said shutting the door to the kids bedroom so that I could be Summer until I was done with the phone call.

"Did you get the pictures?" he asked.

"Yes, it's a beautiful place."

"I want you to come and live with me."

Each time he made a move he left me with a lot to think about. In a way, I was happy that my signals wasn't crossed with this one.

"What about my . . ."

I put my hand over my mouth . . . shit!

"What about your what?" he asked.

I bit my tongue because Mia's secrets were about to be exposed through Summer. Many days I considered walking away from it all. I didn't have any plans so I decided to stay. And here was Phoenix Cooper offering me a way out. I shook my head as if he could see me.

"Nothing. I'm flattered, but what am I suppose to do about my job?"

"Don't worry about all of that. To show you how serious I am I talked to my cousin, the one you met at the barbeque, she works at a hospital and I got you a job. I just need you to say yes."

"I can't its just so sudden."

The fear of change scared the hell out of me. I lived this for five years and I became comfortable in it. Now that he was giving me what I prayed for I was hesitating. I'm not so sure that I ever knew what I wanted, but was using Brian as my disposable scapegoat.

"Time keeps no account of time when you're in love."

My heart ached. Phoenix said that he was in love with me . . . or who he thought I was. I couldn't accept that 'cause it was gained fraudulently.

"Please don't say it, because you don't mean it. You are just in love with who you think I am. I was a fling that got out of hand. How well do we really know each other?"

"That's the thing, I'm dead up. Know this, I don't let anybody in my world and when I do its for real."

"When is this suppose to take place?" I inquired like I was going to take him up on his offer.

"As soon as you're ready."

The front door slammed shut letting me know that Brian was making his special appearance this evening. The risk was too high for me to be exposed so I hung up on him before we could continue the conversation.

My phone lost signal. Text me all the information. You just never know what the future holds. And to answer your question, I'm in love with you too.

"What the hell you been doing all day!" Brian yelled.

I could tell that Brian had been realizing that the grass wasn't greener on the other side. He was miserable. But that wasn't my problem, so I smiled at him.

"Don't smile at me, you nasty pig!" he uttered.

Phoenix kept the smile on my face otherwise I would have been reduced to nothing. He handed me some papers. Brian was not going to break me today.

"I don't want you, these kids or this life. It's papers relinquishing my rights as a father."

I wasn't going to give him the satisfaction of signing the papers and letting him off the hook that easy. I didn't even take the papers.

"Really Brian that's really not necessary." I said calmly.

This was his frequent behavior. One second it was cool, the next second he wanted out.

"That's how I feel! It's because of you and these kids, my life has been turned upside down for five years! Damn, I want out!"

Now he knew how I felt.

"I guess we finally agree on something."

"You condescending bitch!"

"And your mother is another one!"

Brian took the back of his hand and it connected with my mouth. The taste of blood triggered what's been bottled up inside of me for a very long time. With what strength that I had in me, that he didn't snatch away, I stood back and my knee got acquainted with his dick.

"Get the fuck up pussy!"

Brian was shocked and confused as he rolled around the floor balled up in a fetal position holding his manhood. He opened up his mouth and deep moans of pain came out. I was loving watching him squirm like the snake that he was. He stumbled trying to regain his footing, finally pulling himself up on the worn arm of the couch.

"I'm leaving and moving to Dallas with Kera. I'm never coming back. I served my wife with divorce papers today. I'm done with her, you, these damn kids and this life, whether you sign the papers or not!"

The only thing that I could do was laugh at him. As far as I was concerned he was gone a long time ago. I walked over to him and he shielded himself from the unexpected. He had no idea what was coming his way.

My eyes and focus wouldn't leave Brian's hard face. I couldn't do this no more with him. My heart was harden beyond human comprehension. I was mentally fucked and I'd be dammed if I was going to allow him to keep picking me up and dropping me when he damn well pleased. I needed out.

He limped into my bedroom without saying another word and locked the door behind him. What ever I did from this moment on will defiantly effect the rest of my life and the people around me. But that's the thing, I've been putting myself dead last to everyone else and their needs. I finally wanted it to be about me. That wasn't selfish that was life.

I sat on the radiator in my children's bedroom. I went from seeing a clear image of them to only their silhouette as the summer sun faded off into the distance. I shook my head wiping the tears on the back of my hand. I loved them more than life itself but this was even bigger than them.

I stood over Jeremiah, Miranda and Malian looking down on them for what seemed like an eternity. If I stayed any longer I was going to lose my nerve. I bent down closer inhaling their sleepy time lavender lotion remembering their innocence. One at a time I kissed them on their cheek hoping that they would never forget me.

Outside their door I let it all out. I had to get out of here. With only a picture of my babies and a small duffle bag, I got into the waiting cab in front of my complex. As the cab got further my past drifted off with my hard memories. I wanted out and I got it in the way of a stripper. I sacrificed my children to get that freedom that had been snatched away from me a long time ago. The bright side of things is that, I have my man and new life waiting for me in Philly.